Praise for *The Witc*

Suzanne Feldman's uncanny gift for unwrapping ... _ ı
experience to expose our gritty fears, our fierce loves, is
enthrallingly on display in these gleaming stories. With
flashes of sly wit and a refusal to flinch, these beautifully
composed fictions stand with the best that contemporary
fiction has to offer.

— Elise Levine, author of *Say This*

"It was a joy to read Suzanne Feldman's six short stories,
especially the story "The Witch Bottle" for which the collection is named. The story reflects the author's strong
voice, engaging writing, wit, lyricism, humor, and a refresh-
ing second-person point of view. Throughout the collection, Feldman's writing pulls and carries you into vibrant,
colorful worlds alongside textured, layered characters with
stories that make you pause, think, and empathize. As the
winner of the Writers' Publishing House Fiction Prize and a
grant winner from the 2022 Maryland State Arts Individual
Art Award, you're in for a treat with the collection *The
Witch Bottle*. Feldman's writing is sharp, crisp, and flows
flawlessly off the page, creating characters that linger in
your imagination for a long time."

— Arao Ameny, Biography Writer, Editor, Poetry Foundation

Wide-ranging in subject matter and style, these stories are
unwavering in their attention to human passions. Uplifting
and heartbreaking moments go side by side in fiction as in
life, and the punches come from the direction you least
expect. Spending time Suzanne Feldman's world is pure joy.

— Olga Zilberbourg, author of *Like Water and Other Stories*

With writing that is sharp and engaging, *The Witch Bottle* deftly takes its readers through a variety of eras and regions and social settings, at each stop introducing us to new characters who all are desperate to belong. Through the stories in her collection, Suzanne Feldman subtly reminds us that while different periods and circumstances inevitably create their own unique challenges, at heart there is an underlying commonality in human experience that yearns for connection and understanding and meaning. It is being caught at that precise intersection of yearning and expectation that makes each of these stories in *The Witch Bottle* so affecting.

– Adam Braver, author of November 22, 1963 and
Rejoice the Head of Paul McCartney

These are characters who have the courage to live by their ideals in order to honor their art and the values they regard as more important than traditional careers. In this way, Feldman's characters show strength, toughness, and independence.

– Adam Schwartz, Author of Rest of the World

These are all too human stories, with universal themes, revealing frailty and surprising courage. There is much to identify with and reflect upon in these stories and in the wisdom of Ms. Feldman's writings.

Michael T. Tusa Jr author of And Trouble Followed and
A Second Chance at Dancing

With sweeping historical vision and a natural storyteller's charm, Suzanne Feldman takes us on a joyride in *The Witch Bottle*. Each story will surprise in a different way, each story will thrill in manifold ways. What a fantastic collection.

– Matt Gallagher, author of *Empire City* and *Youngblood*

Other books by Suzanne Feldman

Speaking Dreams

Hand of Prophecy

The Annunciate

The Cure For Everything (short story collection)

Absalom's Daughters

Sisters of the Great War

THE WITCH BOTTLE & OTHER STORIES

CONTENTS

Acknowledgments:

The Lapedo Child – *Narrative Magazine*, finalist in *Narrative*'s Spring 2012 Story Contest

Untitled #20 – *Narrative Magazine*, 2013

Self Portraits – *Narrative Magazine*, 2012

The Witch Bottle – *Gargoyle Magazine*, 2017

For all my Witchy Friends

Untitled #20

THE THREE OF US wanted to show our work in the Women's Gallery, which was in a really terrible part of Baltimore, the rent being low and all. This was the '70s, and we were trying to get ourselves recognized in Man's World while at the same time making work that would get us recognized in Woman's World. It was a juggling act, let me tell you. Theresa's work was made of Wonder Bread bags, braided together like the rugs that her grandmother used to make, except her grandmother had used rags. Theresa had wrapped brooms with these masses of plastic and lined a wall with them. Her statement was about history and women's work, although obviously it was *her*story, not *his*.

Genevieve was doing menstrual pieces, which we both agreed would never get her into a mainstream gallery unless she gave them different titles, like *Blood, Blood, and More Blood*. I'd seen horror movies with fewer bodily fluids than she used. No doubt there was a masculine audience for the gore, but she was using tampons as part of her sculptural media, and at the moment she wasn't interested in finding male spectators.

I was, though. I was painting, big broad paintings made by a big broad, as one of my art profs used to say. I liked color. I liked thick, abstract paint. I liked to see color lap over the edges of my canvases. No thin Cézanne washes for me, though I liked Cézanne, even though he was a man. It was hard to find flaws with his work, even through the eyepiece of Feminism, though no doubt he himself was a sexist bastard.

At any rate, the three of us were waiting in the rain for the curator of the Women's Gallery, all of us under a single umbrella standing by the door. Our portfolios were dry, stashed in Theresa's VW bus, which was parked across the street. Like I say, it was a questionable neighborhood and I wondered if the wheels would be gone before we were done here, showing our work to Mynah Hill, seeing if we passed muster and could show in the Women's Gallery.

The front of the gallery was a big papered-over plate glass window. Word had it that the place had once been a beauty salon, which would have been coolly ironic, if it were true. To me, the building looked like a revamped gas station, which also might have a hint of irony. I pushed the doorbell again and banged on the door for good measure. The knob rattled from the other side and Genevieve said, "*Finally,*" as Mynah Hill pulled the door open to us, the gray street, and the rain.

Mynah was a skinny old woman with long gray hair and paint-covered jeans. She was, as we all were in those days, braless, but it looked more comfortable on some of us than on others.

"Hi," she said, "where's your work?"

Theresa gestured to the van, and Mynah said, "Well, don't leave it in there! Bring it in before everything disappears."

It struck me that thieves probably wouldn't be interested in our objets d'art, because after all, they were thieves, not critics. Our hubcapless wheels were worth more than wrapped brooms, tampon sculptures, or my attempts at grand-mastery painting. Still, we scurried off into the downpour to retrieve our stuff and get it in before the colors ran.

We set our work up on a low platform, the kind a band would perform on. Mynah brought us tea in handmade mugs and we sat on an old oriental carpet that was scattered with pillows. On the walls were posters from previous shows, shows in New York, shows in Fresno, shows wherever Mynah had been networking with Women's Spaces. We had a lot of, possibly too much, respect for her opinions. I could tell by the way she gripped her hot mug that Genevieve was prepared to live or die by what she heard in this room. Theresa, who had shown elsewhere, in galleries where the *her*storical aspects of her brooms had been eclipsed by the sheer oddity of the objects, would be a little more circumspect, but probably not much more than me. *This* was where we wanted to show. We wanted a female audience for our female work, women who would see it and judge it for what it was, not for what it seemed to be in some man's eyes. We'd put a lot of effort into making things that No Man would ever think of creating, and we were proud of our pieces. It remained to be seen if our work would convey all that in this particular environment. I was especially nervous because abstract paintings were often just abstract paintings, without a shred of discernible politics.

"The tampons," said Mynah, "are tremendous."

Genevieve let out her breath in relief but disguised it by blowing on her tea. "Thanks," she said.

"The wrapped broom," said Mynah. "Interesting."

"I have a dozen of them," said Theresa. "I line them up against a wall. They create a kind of environment."

"I like that," said Mynah. "I like the idea of that." She sipped tea and studied mine, which was three feet tall and a foot and a half wide, slathered with a variety of blues and emerald greens, bits of white peeking through, and just a touch of alizarin crimson from where I'd let the primed canvas show. That was the thin part, my tribute to Cézanne. I almost hoped Mynah wouldn't notice, but I knew she would. My work was completely unlike Genevieve's and Theresa's. Mine was compromised by my desire to get into male-run galleries. I could see now, my work lined up next to the other two, that it was something that didn't belong. I felt tears come up behind my eyes and my throat began to burn. I took in a hot mouthful of tea to make myself snap out of it. I was a big broad. I could handle anything this woman said about my painting, and anything, by way of that, that she would say about me.

"The painting," said Mynah, "should speak for itself, but it doesn't."

Theresa and Genevieve widened their eyes and looked sideways at me for my reaction.

"It might need a written component," said Mynah. "I love the color and the format. I like the hint of crimson, like it's bleeding, just a little. But it may be too . . . I don't know. Too abstract for the kind of vibe we want in this gallery."

"I could add a written component," I said. "It's an emotional piece, though. I wouldn't want to just, you know, explain what it is. I want the viewer to come to her own conclusion."

Mynah nodded slowly, sipping. "Maybe just a card on the side. What's the title?"

"It's untitled," I said, too quickly. I could have come up with something if I'd given myself half a minute to think.

"Well, you'll need a title," said Mynah. "And it looks to me like a process piece. Maybe even a paragraph or two about your process."

I nodded, not sure what she meant. *Process* usually meant that a thing turned into another thing after being made, the process being part of its becoming. Genevieve's tampons processed from being wet to dry, when the color of her fluids changed to look even more like blood. My painting wasn't processing into anything. It had become all it was going to be.

"Is it still wet by any chance?" said Mynah.

Alarm bells should have gone off in my head at this point, but instead I nodded like an idiot. "Just a little. In the thickest parts."

"You should write in the paint," said Mynah. "Put words on there. They don't have to be really big." She made a tiny shape with her fingers. "You know. Just a paragraph or two, written in the paint. Make it part of the composition, the process, before it's too dry."

I tried—really tried—to decide that this was a good idea.

"Maybe on a different piece," I said.

"No, I like this one," said Mynah. "I think with a little tweaking it would fit in just fine. These others"—she gestured at the wrapped broom and the tampons—"they're in. Yours is the one I'm not sure about."

I wanted to ask her what she thought I should write. I wanted to tell her I wasn't about to adulterate my blues and emerald greens with scratched-in letters about a process that wasn't even there, but I didn't say any of those things. I especially didn't say that I thought this particular piece could probably get into a man-owned gallery just exactly the way it was. Which made me doubt its Feminist quality, which made me seriously consider what Mynah had just said.

"Um," I said. "Do you have some paper and a pencil I could borrow? I'll have to decide what to put on there."

She hopped right up and got me a clipboard with a piece of typing paper on it and a pencil tied to it with a long piece of string. I put down my tea and made myself *not* ask her what she thought I should write.

Meanwhile, Genevieve and Theresa were silently congratulating each other, trying to be cool about it. Getting into this gallery was no mean feat, a real résumé builder, especially inside the Women's Community.

As I sat on the floor, surrounded by cushions, the tethered pencil poised above the paper, which was as frightening as a blank canvas, Mynah dropped down next to me. She was a spry old thing. There was no *oomph* as she sat, no creakiness. I felt huge next to her.

"Title it first," she said, as though it was obvious I was struggling with my unexpected assignment. "Give it a name that sounds like heat. All those cool colors and that one slice of crimson. You could call it *Burn* and then give it a series number. How many of these have you done?"

"Like this? Maybe four."

"That's not enough," said Mynah. "Call it *Burn Number 19*—or *20*, that might sound better."

"But," I said, "I only have four or five. What if someone asks to see the other fifteen?"

"Just tell them the others were trash," said Mynah, and patronizingly, she added, "lots of artists have series with numbers missing. Not everything you're going to do is gold."

"But fifteen trash paintings?" I held the pencil away from the paper. *Burn?* I didn't like it at all. "Why couldn't I call it *Untitled 5?*"

"Because then it doesn't sound like you have an extensive portfolio. Just write," she said impatiently, and I wrote down *Untitled 19.* "That'll do, I guess. Now tell me about your process."

"Well," I said, "I like Cézanne, but I wanted to paint in opposition to him, with thick paint on a vertical format. But I still wanted to maintain some of his landscape elements."

"So you're taking on the so-called Father of Modern Art. Good. But you need to sound more militant. None of this good-girl variations-on-a-theme kind of thing. You're not riffing, you're rebelling. I mean," she made a wide, almost dismissive gesture at my work, "just look at the red slash." She narrowed her eyes. "Now that I look again, I feel that it may need to be bigger. You don't want to *understate.*"

I felt like she wanted to rip the pencil out of my hand and write the whole thing herself.

Genevieve cleared her throat. "Laurie," she said to me, "are you sure you want to make those kinds of changes? They're awfully severe."

I hesitated. Theresa cocked her head, concern for the integrity of my artistic statement in her eyes.

"No," I said, "it's all right. I mean . . ." I looked at Mynah. "You're saying if I make these changes, you'll show my work."

"This particular piece," said Mynah.

I shrugged at my friends. "It's fine," I said, knowing perfectly well that it wasn't.

Later they watched as I wrote essentially what Mynah had dictated to me about the process I had supposedly gone through, into the flesh of my thick, not-quite-dry paint. What she wanted me to say about Cézanne and the patriarchy wouldn't quite fit on the canvas, which, due to the writing, now had a wriggly and cracked surface texture. So we untied the pencil from the clipboard and continued "my" diatribe onto the gallery wall where my ruined painting would hang. At one point she actually took the pencil from my hand and corrected my spelling and then added a few words with an exclamation mark. We placed my piece beside the writing. Theresa and Genevieve held it up on either side so we could see it in context. If you stood far enough back, the painting still looked intact. Any closer than six feet, though, and the illusion of cohesion disappeared.

But Mynah seemed thrilled. She shook our hands as we left and gave us a clenched-fist salute as we piled into the VW, which was still in one piece and sitting in the rain just where we'd left it.

Theresa started the engine and pulled away from the curb.

Genevieve said, "I can't believe you let her do that."

"Do what?" I said defensively.

"You let her destroy a perfectly good painting," said Theresa.

"Obviously it wasn't good enough to get in," I said, "not without some—what did she say? Tweaking."

"That was more than a tweak," said Genevieve.

"More like a yank," said Theresa.

"More like an ax murder," said Genevieve. "You let her make you *write* on it."

"I didn't *let* her make me do anything," I said, but obviously I had and there was no denying it. I looked out the window at the crummy wet houses and broken-down cars we were passing. "All right," I said. "You tell me what I should've done."

"Maybe it wasn't so important to get into that show," said Theresa.

"Too late," I said. "I'm in. And so are you."

"You could've taken that painting to any gallery. Not even a man would have made you write all over it."

"Maybe it wasn't that good a painting," I said. "Maybe what she did was the right thing. Maybe that's the direction I should be going in. Thick paint with manifesto. Maybe I should do one for each of the old masters. *That'd* be a series. I could get at least twenty paintings out of that, even if I had to trash fifteen."

"I can't believe she said that to you," said Theresa.

"It's like I could've brought in a canvas with red splashed on it, called it *Menstruation,* and that would have been fine. I should have hung a tampon from it," I said, but Genevieve bristled.

"Don't trivialize," she said in a warning tone.

"I'm not," I said, but I was because I was high on the destruction of my perfectly good painting. I was rolling. "I should have framed it in Wonder Bread bags," I said. "I wonder what she'll do with the rest of your brooms when you bring them in, Theresa—paint them red? Insist on generic wrapping?"

"She's not changing *my* work," said Theresa. "She already accepted it."

"Maybe we shouldn't have left our stuff there," I said. "Who knows what the hell she's doing to it right now."

Theresa and Genevieve, in the front, glanced at each other.

"It's two weeks to the show," I said. "A lot can happen in two weeks."

Theresa slowed and stopped at a green light. "Shit," she said. "We should go back and get everything."

Someone honked behind us.

"Not mine," I said. "Don't turn around on my account. I've been elevated already. What more can she do? I even know where mine's going to be hanging."

"Jesus Christ," said Genevieve, and Theresa swung the Volkswagen around in the middle of the intersection.

Mynah was so irritated that Theresa and Genevieve didn't trust her with their artwork that she kicked them out of the show before it even started. On opening night my vandalized painting was the centerpiece of the exhibit, and when people asked me about it, I explained about the title, the fifteen or so rejected paintings, my relationship with Cézanne, and my process of leaving him and everything masculine about him behind in the form of a trailing paragraph. An art dealer was there, a man who thought of himself as exceptionally liberated. He was so liberated that he told me frankly over wine and cheese that he didn't especially like the piece but that he was interested in my portfolio since, without the writing, he thought the painting had quite a lot of promise. I tried to be demure. I tried not to be smug, but I failed at both. I grinned at him and got his card and made myself not wave it in Mynah's face when she came over to me, beaming with a plastic cup full of wine.

"It's such a supportive space," she said, "don't you think? Wouldn't you agree?"

"Yes, indeed," I said. "I couldn't agree with you more."

Self Portraits

THE DAY RAY BROKE UP WITH HER was the day Lisa cut off her hair, all of it, with the shears she kept in her tiny kitchen. She cut without a mirror, just kept going until there was nothing left for the scissors to get a purchase on and the brown kitchen floor was scattered with snakes of black hair. She went into the bathroom to see what she'd accomplished. The uneven dark brush of a crew cut wasn't enough. She took Ray's razor and shaved her scalp until her hair was nothing but a shadow and his razor was ruined.

And then, since there was hair all over the apartment and the next step would be to weepingly clean it up, she sat down at her easel and started a new self-portrait to add to the dozens already leaning against the walls of her microscopic Baltimore apartment. She put on one of his suit jackets and included that in the picture. She didn't look a thing like him; he was tall and blond, she was short and, as he had said once, swarthy—and that was exactly how she painted herself. Bald and swarthy, enveloped in the baggy jacket.

It got dark outside and the background wasn't done. Instead of turning on the lights and finishing, she left the painting as it was, with the jacket done and her own features 90 percent blocked in. She got all his other clothes, took off the jacket, and threw everything out the window onto the sidewalk three stories below. Then, when it was too dark to do anything else but turn on the lights, she swept up her hair into a pillowcase, sobbing the whole time, because as faithless and full of shit as Ray was, she had genuinely been in love with him. But in all honesty, she wasn't crying about that. She was crying about how stupid she felt for being so upset.

THE NEXT DAY she finished the painting without a mirror. She'd done so many self-portraits that it was easier to add expression when she didn't have to look at her own sadness. She just painted what she felt and it came out that way. When she was finished, she turned the painting to the wall to let it dry and so it could make any magical changes that might happen while she wasn't looking at it. She took a shower and put on some clean clothes. She put on a baseball cap and had to tighten it up. She didn't look in the mirror before she left to go out on the street.

HER FRIENDS FROM ART SCHOOL, Kelly, Marie, Justine, and Neary, who had graduated and gone into waitressing careers, often hung out together at one of the coffee shops, letting other women wait on them for a change while they smoked cigarettes and drank espresso in preparation for their afternoon and evening shifts. They still painted, or sculpted or drew, but none of them had shown, like Lisa. None of them had sold, like she had. None of them could call themselves truly starving artists because they had jobs that fed them. Lisa'd had to give away her cat because she couldn't afford cat food. She had given the cat, whose name was Harold, to Kelly, who was sitting alone at an outdoor table with her cigarette and a white cup of espresso with a slice of lemon peel in the saucer. It was a three-dollar drink. Kelly worked as a barista at a Starbucks by day and as a hostess at a fancy French restaurant by night. She could afford a three-dollar drink. Lisa sat down across from her. The waitress saw Lisa and turned to get her what she always ordered, which was an egg sandwich with a slice of American cheese and a cup of coffee. It was a two-dollar meal, with a fifty-cent tip.

"Interestingly enough," said Kelly, "I saw some man picking up a pile of clothes from the sidewalk underneath your window this morning."

"Did he look like Ray?" said Lisa. "Because otherwise some homeless guy hit the mother lode."

"Looked like Ray," said Kelly. She acted like she hadn't noticed the shaved head in front of her. She took a drag from her cigarette instead and offered it to Lisa, then withdrew it. Lisa had given up smoking because it was a habit that cost more than paint, when you got right down to it.

"Don't tell me any more," said Lisa. "I don't ever want to know any more. He was cheating on me. He was cheating on me with a *junior* from art school."

The waitress brought the sandwich and the coffee, which was bottomless. "I almost didn't recognize you," said the waitress. She was older, a little bit nosy, as she had a right to be, since Lisa and Kelly were here almost every morning. "Man trouble?" she guessed.

"Or head lice," said Kelly blandly. The waitress gave a twitch like she believed it, then let out a nervous laugh, like whatever it was, man trouble or lice, it was catching. Another customer came in and she trotted away.

"You really, really didn't have to cut off your hair," said Kelly.

"I put it in a pillowcase," said Lisa. "For luck or something. Can I borrow your vacuum? I can't get it all with a broom and a dustpan."

"Well, of course, honey. You have a key. Come over this afternoon and pick it up."

"I did do a painting," said Lisa.

"Self-portrait as a concentration camp victim?" said Kelly. She crushed the cigarette. "If you get any skinnier, that's what you'll look like."

"I was thinking chemotherapy. I haven't done the background yet. I was thinking tubes and wires. Like a life-support system."

"He wasn't a life-support system," said Kelly. "He was anything but. If I think about it long enough I'll be able to tell you what he was, but the word that comes to mind is *sleaze*."

"I don't know how to paint *sleaze*."

"One day," said Kelly, "I'm going to become an advice columnist and then I'll get paid for saying to people, 'stay away from that cheating bastard.' You know he was just too good-looking."

"Right," said Lisa. "I should only go for the ugly ones."

"Obviously not what I meant," said Kelly. "I wish you hadn't done that to your beautiful hair. Don't you have an opening in three weeks or something?"

"Two and a half."

"Let me know if you want a wig or something. It's kind of freaky. Let me see." She reached for the hat and cocked it to one side without waiting for permission. "Wow. In a couple of weeks you might have a decent fuzz, but I don't know…"

"There's nothing I can do about it now." Lisa pushed the hat back into place. "Anyway, I'm already using it in a painting. Maybe I'll make a series about how it grows back in."

"Give me a little of what you cut off and I can use it in something of mine." Kelly's work was embroidery and extraordinarily time-consuming. Lisa could easily imagine her hair sewn into whatever Kelly came up with, but her piece would take months, and by the time Kelly was done, Lisa's hair would be back.

"What you need is better hats," said Kelly. "There's the cutest antique clothing place by Starbucks. I'll see if I can find you a snood, or a pillbox hat, or something like Jackie Kennedy would wear."

"Ray's a cheating shit," said Lisa dryly, "not a dead president."

"Still," said Kelly. "Hats. Series. Keep thinking series. At least make him good for something." She put a couple of dollars on the table, got up, and put her arms around Lisa. "Oh, sweetie, I'm so sorry he was a rat. I've had so many of them I should've seen it in him, but he seemed like such a nice guy."

Which made Lisa's eyes feel gritty and hot.

"Gotta go," said Kelly. "Come see me at work today if you need to cry your eyes out. I'll get you a frappé for free."

AFTER THAT, the sandwich seemed tasteless. The coffee was too hot to have any flavor, but at least it *was* hot. It was early October, almost too cold to be sitting outside with an egg and cheese sandwich and no one to talk to. She wondered where the rest of her friends were, Marie, Justine, and Neary, all of whom subsisted on tips on good nights and minimum wage the rest of the time. Lisa drank more coffee and frowned at the cars passing by. What if Ray called and apologized for the cheating—possibly just the tip of the iceberg of cheating—what would she say? The advice Kelly gave in her advice columnist persona wasn't so far off. Lisa read Dear Abby in the *Baltimore Sun* whenever she could find a free copy. That and the comics. The news didn't interest her because it seemed like the news was the same all the time and shouldn't be called "news." It was like the advice columns in a lot of ways, and in a lot of ways like breaking up with Ray. The same thing happened all the time. People hated their bridesmaid dresses but didn't want to say anything. People hated their mothers-in-law but had to deal with them somehow. Trusted boyfriends cheated, *skillfully* cheated with malice aforethought, and it was nothing new. It was only new to *her*. And now there was this boyfriendless landscape, which, frankly, she'd probably been standing in for quite some time without knowing it.

Had he been a nice guy? The sex had been good. It was the sweaty kind, like hot oil sliding between them, the kind where they peeled themselves away from each other afterward, separating long enough to cool off for the next round. But was that it? He was a painter too—he showed at bigger galleries than she did. In her deepest suspicions of herself, she wondered if she had connected with him in order to make a connection with his gallerists. But that wasn't right. He'd said constructive things about her work, made good suggestions, and he'd been fun to go out with. Maybe on some level, especially after a year of going out with no word of long-term plans, she should have been suspicious of his motivations, but to be cheated on with a *junior* in *art school* who was probably just coming up with the same old ideas as everyone else in art school—what did that mean about her own work? Did it mean that he felt threatened by the quality of it and had to move on? Because there were two things you couldn't separate in a relationship, and that was the artist from his or her work. She'd always thought his was good, sophisticatedly abstract—a nice counterbalance to her realism—not threatening or competitive in any way. So if he was cheating on her, he was cheating on her paintings as well, which meant that somewhere in there was a lie about his opinion of her quality, skill, talent, whatever. Something even more deeply insulting than sleeping with someone else—it was the cheating on her work that hurt the most. And what hurt the most about that was that she didn't really realize how much she'd depended on his opinion until this very minute, at this chilly table in front of this familiar coffee shop. She was so ferociously glad she'd shaved her head and thrown his things out the window, she burst into hot tears right there, and was crying so hard when the waitress came to clear off Kelly's coffee cup that she put her arm around Lisa's shoulder and murmured *there, there,* just like a mother or a really good friend.

INDEED HIS CLOTHES were off the sidewalk when she got back to her apartment, not a trace of him or his boxer shorts. He was lucky his paintings were elsewhere. She would have flung them out the window as well, no matter how great his work was.

She went up to her apartment and put the background into the self-portrait of herself in her ex-boyfriend's jacket—not tubes and wires but coils of black hair all over the floor.

LISA HAD NO DOUBT that Ray would be able to find a better place to live than her apartment, and probably a better girlfriend to live with, in no time. He was tall and blond, after all, not your typical artsy-fartsy guy who always smelled of turpentine. They'd met at a Halloween party a year ago when she was dressed as a sword maiden, and he was dressed as a prisoner in an orange jumpsuit. The jumpsuit was smeared with oil paint, which made him look less like an escapee and more like someone who hadn't put any thought into a costume and had come straight from his studio to the dance. He'd at least stenciled a prisoner number over his heart and *Folsom* over the back. Lisa assumed that this meant he listened to Johnny Cash, whom she'd recently discovered, and so when the music changed, she danced on over to him and in an act of bravado, which was very unlike her, asked why he wasn't wearing Folsom Prison blues instead of orange. It took him a minute to get the reference, which should have been a warning sign—he'd barely heard of Johnny Cash, she found out later—but he laughed at the joke and gave her a friendly shrug which turned into a dance move, and then, what the hell, they were dancing, and no matter what the DJ put on next, they kept dancing. She got his name and came to the conclusion he had come with *guy* friends, not a girlfriend, which she couldn't quite believe because he was so painterly that artiness practically oozed off him. Another warning sign she should have seen. They went out for drinks and candy afterward at the Mount Royal Tavern, the Art Institute's dive bar, the one with the big painting behind the bar of the nudes, entitled *Starting Gate at Pimlico*. He talked about his art, which she realized she'd seen through the windows of Grimaldis Gallery downtown, which made her a little nervous, but she liked the way his hair fell over his forehead and she liked the way he talked about art, asking her opinions and then listening to what she had to say. Not too far into the evening, she realized she would wear high heels for him if they ever went to a place that required such a thing. Heels were what she used as a yardstick against possible relationships. She had a pair but rarely wore them to anything but friends' weddings. Even in high school the Heel Rule had been effective. Friends who had since gotten married had introduced her to it. If you weren't willing to put your feet through hell for a guy, why bother?

On their first date he took her to a restaurant down the street from Grimaldis. On the second he took her to his opening. She wore heels both times. On their third date, he showed her his studio, which was in the old warehouse at the end of the Howard Street Bridge, right next to the crab house. They had sex on the cheap lawn furniture he kept in his studio, totally silent because there were other people in the next room, behind nothing more than a plywood wall.

Another warning sign that she had utterly ignored. How easy it was for him to be so quiet during sex in the studio. Studios were chick magnets. Everyone knew that. How many just like her had he had in there, while his expressive abstracts dried on their easels all around them? She was so deliriously happy about it when he moved in, that keeping their studio spaces separate seemed perfectly reasonable. There wasn't room for his big gestural works in her tiny apartment anyway. And he seemed deliriously happy too. She didn't know until a lot later that his apartment lease had expired at the end of November and, if nothing else, he needed a place to crash.

He'd even fooled her girlfriends, who showed up, glowing, with their own boyfriends at Ray's openings, making special arrangements to get away from their waitressing shifts and exchanging their sneakers for elegant shoes.

Now what bothered her—besides the cheating—was his level of sincerity and her level of stupidity. Was he such a good actor that he could pretend for almost an entire *year* that he was in love with her? If that was the case, he was in the wrong profession. If that was the case, he should have gotten an Emmy instead of gallery space at Grimaldis.

SHE STARTED the next painting for her upcoming show. She was supposed to have a dozen paintings. She had eight, not including the one from last night. She wasn't prepared to turn it around and look at it yet, not ready to commit to it. The one she meant to work on was another self-portrait—it was what she was known for—a portrait of the artist as a young woman, although now, bald, she might as well title it *Portrait of the Artist as a Young Man*. Instead she brushed in the big outline of her building and painted a heap of clothes lying on the sidewalk. She added a figure, like someone who had jumped out the window, lying next to it. Then she painted two more figures in midair, as though falling in stop-motion. Then she swirled clouds around the whole thing. She put in her own apartment window and added the self-portrait—herself framed in the window looking down at the falling, and fallen, bodies.

Kelly, Marie, Justine, and Neary came over after their shifts that night, which meant that her friends showed up at midnight with six-packs and pizza. They stayed for a couple of hours offering advice but limited sympathy, Lisa thought, as though they had discussed Ray among themselves earlier and decided he was a bad risk for her. By the time they left it was two in the morning and Lisa rolled into bed, alone again but too tired and beery to care or even to brush her teeth.

HER SCALP itched. It itched so much she wondered if it meant something was about to happen, and that was when Ray knocked on the door.

She looked at him through the peephole and wondered if she should just pretend not to be at home. He knocked again and stuck his eye up against the peephole as though he could see in from the outside. Which made her angry but also made her feel a weird, furious form of affection for him. So she opened the door fast, so he wouldn't have time to step back.

"Whoa," he said. "I didn't think you were home."

"What do you want?"

"Nothing," he said. "I have these. They're yours." He held out a fistful of paintbrushes. They were her expensive ones, the sables.

She took them without touching his hand or looking into his eyes. "Thanks. I was wondering where they were." Which was a lie. She'd forgotten she'd lent them to him.

"Look," he said, "I know I'm a complete shit, but do you want me to come to your show? I want Beth Grimaldis to see your stuff, and she won't come unless I say something to her."

She wanted to say, *"Only a complete shit would blackmail me with that kind of exposure."* Instead, she said, "That would be nice of you." What was he to her now—a professional contact? She wanted to punch him, but she wanted Grimaldis more.

He blinked at her and she realized he was noticing her shaved scalp under the baseball cap for the first time.

"Your hair," he started, and she slammed the door in his face as hard as she could.

Then she went into the bathroom and cried over the expensive sable brushes, which he had been using for months to create expensive masterpieces that would sell out of his expensive gallery like hotcakes.

HE AT LEAST had the decency not to bring his art school junior with him to her opening. He at least had the decency to make sure that Beth Grimaldis looked at Lisa's strongest work and divert her from the rest.

Kelly, Marie, Justine, and Neary, each in heels and skirts, sipped cheap champagne from plastic flutes. Two and a half weeks of growth had resulted in a dark, rough fuzz on Lisa's head, and though she had been tempted by Kelly's offer of a wig or a snood, whatever that was, she'd decided to go bareheaded, in flats and a skirt. A buzz cut and heels just didn't go together. People gathered around the haircut self-portrait and nodded knowledgably, gathering insight on the artist's process, or whatever. In all, Lisa thought, there were probably five pieces here that she was really pleased with. The others, both pre- and post-Ray, seemed weak, and she felt a bit queasy that she'd had the chutzpah to put them up at all. Better to have plain white walls than some of these things up where people could see them. She tried to shake those thoughts out of her head. People came over to congratulate her. Neary, who had seen hardly any of this work, thoughtfully praised the series aspect of the self-portraits.

"I can see the breakup," she said. "Your colors get harder after you kicked him out. It's like you were steeling yourself."

Finally, Ray brought Beth Grimaldis over and introduced her, although everyone in Baltimore's art sphere knew this woman and her wild shoes and matching eyeglasses.

"I don't think I can offer you a whole show," said Beth Grimaldis while Kelly, Marie, Justine, and Neary tried not to crowd around. "But I like the haircut piece. I'd like to hang that one in my gallery next month."

Ray just stood there with his hands in his pockets. He hadn't dressed at all for the event. He might as well have been wearing his orange jumpsuit from Halloween. He smiled as if he had put this very idea into Grimaldis's mind. Who knew—maybe he had.

"Thank you so much," said Lisa with as much feeling as she could. "That's such an honor."

"Ray's really advocated for you," she said. "I can see why. Some of the work is uneven, but your series is strong and I like the direction you're going."

Even though she had heard this from dozens of art profs, it sounded different coming out of Beth Grimaldis's mouth. It sounded solid. She tried not to look at Ray.

"Thank you so much," Lisa said again.

"Bring it by when your show comes down," said Beth Grimaldis, "but put it in a better frame." She handed Lisa a card with a framer's name on it. It was an expensive place. She knew Ray took his work there. "Tell him I sent you—he'll give you a good discount."

"I will," said Lisa.

Beth Grimaldis turned and vanished into the crowd. Lisa expected Ray to trail after her, but instead he gave her a winning smile—as if he was winning and had just won something fantastic for her as well. And now he expected to be thanked.

Lisa ran a hand over her bristly head. "Thanks," she said. "That was nice of you."

"You deserve it," said Ray with great magnanimity.

She didn't want to say more, but if she didn't he would never do anything for her again. She hated that she was beholden to him. She hated that he was so far ahead of her in his career, that he was so blond, so tall, so enviable. She hated that his new girlfriend probably wanted the same things from him that Lisa wanted right now. She hated that her relationship with him seemed far from over. She deeply hated that she felt like this in what should be a moment of triumph.

"Maybe she'll hang us next to each other," she said as nicely as she could.

He lit up at that, not boyishly but as if the idea appealed to him on a clear level of manipulation.

BACK IN HER APARTMENT, she primed another canvas, scrubbing gesso into the stiff white fabric. This was a big one, thirty-six inches by forty-eight, by far the largest of the self-portraits she had done. Outside the wind was picking up as a late-November storm moved in. The air felt electric. She felt it in her hands. She had a title for this one already. *Place Your Bets* was what she would call it, and somehow it would relate to the tarred-over *Starting Gate* in the Mount Royal Tavern.

She set a fan in front of the canvas to force the drying and sketched herself as a full-length nude on separate pieces of paper. Nude wasn't something she normally did. Not out of modesty, it just wasn't something that fit into her vision, but now, *now*, exposed at Grimaldis Gallery, exposed altogether, getting exposure. It just seemed time. She touched the canvas and found it cool and sticky. Just another half hour and it would be right. It was midnight now. By morning she would have the bones of the drawing on the canvas. She pulled a cheap, long mirror out of the closet and set it near the easel. This mirror was made of plastic and distorted everything it reflected. It didn't matter. She stripped off her clothes and stood in front of her own bowed image. Behind her was an open window. She could have pulled the shade down, but if all the world was going to see her naked, then modesty and privacy wouldn't matter now. Once she had modeled for an art class when she was really broke and workmen had been washing the windows of the studio, staring in at her. The instructor had finally pulled the blinds down. When she walked out afterward, fully clothed, she saw them again, recognized them, but they didn't recognize her. It was a strange disguise, nudity. Once, back in school, she had been painting another woman, one of the Institute's regular models. The janitors had sauntered past the open door of the studio and smirked at the model, who defended herself in the only way she could without moving. She shut her eyes.

Now she stood eyes open, naked in front of the big canvas, armed with her sables, framed by the open window. She turned on music. The smell of turpentine and linseed oil enveloped her. A great song came on and she began to paint.

IT WASN'T FINISHED by morning, but she hadn't expected it to be. She took a shower at six and put on her pajamas. By seven she was in bed.

AROUND NINE, when she was in the depths of sleep, someone knocked on her door. It was Kelly with two cups of coffee and a white paper bakery bag.

"You weren't at the coffee place," she said. "I just wanted to see if you were okay." She saw the painting. "Oh," she said. "Sorry. You were up all night, I guess."

"What do you think?"

"Well," said Kelly, "it's big and naked. It reminds me of something."

"The *Starting Gate* in the tavern?"

She snapped her fingers. "That sexist thing. I knew I'd seen that angle of ass somewhere. So what's this—a riff or a parody? Never mind—I shouldn't make you talk about it." She set the coffee down on the only table in the apartment and opened the bag. "Doughnuts," she said, "or do you want to go back to sleep?"

"Nah," she said, "I can sleep later."

Kelly settled herself on one of the kitchen chairs and helped herself to a doughnut. "It's such a sleazy angle," she said. "Is this your answer to Ray's abstractions? Booty realism?"

"I wanted it to be revealing," she said. "Not revealed."

"Exposed?"

"Yeah," she said. "Naked instead of nude."

"Oh," said Kelly, "I think you got that. I'm not even sure you need to do much more to it. More might be overkill."

"I have to put the face in, though." Right now the face was just a quick brushstroke showing the angle of the eyebrow meeting the bridge of the nose.

"Maybe you don't," said Kelly. "Maybe you should leave it alone for a couple of days. Maybe making it a self-portrait is too much information."

"Too revealing?"

"Way revealing. You might as well walk naked down the street. Right now it's a naked you because everyone knows it's you. You don't have to hit your audience over the head."

"Not even Grimaldis?"

"Especially not Grimaldis." Kelly lifted her Styrofoam cup up in a toast. "Congrats. You're done."

She wasn't sure how much she agreed, but she tapped cups with Kelly and decided it was time to start something new.

SHE DID A SERIES of nudes over the next two weeks, some fully fleshed out, some just barely more than the brushstrokes it took to suggest the naked female form. Some she covered over with thin paint, just enough to give the indication of something seen through a curtain. Some she covered more thickly, so that only parts of the complete whole were visible under the edges. Some of these she scraped away until both the figure and the texture of the canvas were visible. Some she redrew on top of the original in a different pose. When she had a dozen, she lined them all up along her walls. It was three in the morning. She made a fresh pot of coffee and spent the rest of the morning rearranging them in different sequences until she knew how to make them a coherent series. Then she took off her clothes and painted until noon.

Kelly came every morning with coffee and an egg sandwich. Sometimes she came with groceries. Sometimes she cooked while Lisa painted, sometimes they just talked. Sometimes they talked about Ray, but not often and mostly within the context of Grimaldis Gallery.

"You haven't been outside this apartment in weeks, have you," said Kelly, more as a statement of fact than a question. "Ray's show's going up at Grimaldis. You can tear yourself away from all this and go see his stuff, can't you?"

She agreed, took a shower, shaved her legs, and put on a dress and her parka. It was almost Christmas, she realized, when they went outside into the evening. Baltimore was decked out in red and green lights. Even in the gallery district there were wreaths and twinkling white lights, all arranged so as not to look tacky.

Ray's work was in the window of Grimaldis. She recognized it right away, even though it was new enough that she hadn't seen it before. His faux desert landscapes with their sky-blue cliffs and earthy ochers were unmistakable. They were long, narrow pieces, like her big figure paintings, as though they had been laid down on their sides. For a second she had a flash of understanding that these weren't landscapes at all but thinly disguised paintings of his new girlfriend, lying naked across an expanse of rumpled sheets and blankets. The thought made her furious when she pictured the work he'd done when the two of them were together. *Starting Gate at Pimlico,* she thought, was at least recognizable, on display without pretense of arty camouflage. It was a dirty painting without any apologies and had hung just so in the bar for years. Not these licentious landscapes. She hated that he had probably painted some of them with her sables.

"What's the matter?" said Kelly.

"Nothing," she said. "They're good, aren't they?"

Kelly feigned a yawn. "If you like desert-looking stuff. Let's go in."

The gallery wasn't full, but there were enough people there to make her think of an opening crowd. She realized she was hungry and glanced around for the wine and cheese but there was just the crowd, no food, only money changing hands as people invested in Ray and whoever else was lucky enough to show in this gallery at this time of year. Envy made her chest hurt. Her one painting wasn't scheduled to go up until after the holidays, during slump season for sales. It made her feel unimportant and faintly duped, even though the cachet of being in the Grimaldis stable—even just one painting—was undeniable.

"I'm starving," she said to Kelly. "Have you seen enough? Let's go get something to eat."

KELLY TOOK HER to the Greek place not far from the Art Institute and bought her a gyro and a Coke. Lisa ate too fast and her stomach hurt afterward. She wanted to ask Kelly if she thought she was overreacting, feeling ripped off by Grimaldis, utterly betrayed by Ray, even though both of them seemed, on the face of it, to be supportive, even encouraging. But she was afraid of what Kelly would say, either positive or negative, and that the leftover feelings of her opinions would then impinge on the paintings, so precariously arranged in her apartment. They were delicate things at this stage. Even the ideas behind them, which made them hold together as a unit, seemed too fragile to sustain themselves by way of a spoken explanation. What bothered her most was that she wanted Ray's opinion, and the more she thought about that the angrier she became. Kelly would have laughed if Lisa had said any of this aloud, and called it dependence or, worse, labeled it a kind of female weakness. In the same room as the paintings, Kelly's laugh might have torn the tender fabric that held the idea of the series together. Which was nothing compared to what Ray might say, depending on his mood. But she was stuck, and when she hugged Kelly good-bye at the front door of her building, she knew she was going to call Ray as soon as she got upstairs.

What if he wouldn't come? What if he thought what she really wanted was breakup sex? What if he laughed at her work? She stood in the center of the room, surrounded by her own image, like a circle of dancers, and felt only slightly stronger. Before she had time to talk herself out of it, she took out her phone and called.

He answered on the first ring.

"Lisa?"

She hesitated and then let the words come out on their own.

"I need your opinion on something."

"Sure," he said. "What?"

"I need you to come over and look at these paintings."

"Right now?"

She looked at the clock by her bed. It was past eleven. "Yeah," she said. "Right now." By daylight she knew she would lose her nerve, both to ask questions and to hear his answers. "Look," she said, "I don't forgive you. But I need to know what you think."

There was a long silence and she strained to hear the new girlfriend's voice in the background, but there was nothing, just Ray deciding whether or not to come over. "All right," he said. "I'll be there in twenty minutes."

She hung up and fought the urge to neaten up the place before he got there. Her stupid heart crammed in on itself and made her stomach hurt even more. What would he say, anyway—what was she hoping for? What if he said something negative—or even laughed? After all, what was more trite and overdone than the nude female form?

When he knocked, she was scrubbing her brushes in the sink. Her hands smelled of turpentine.

She opened the door, and he stepped into the circle of the full-length nudes. He turned around once to see them all. "Whoa," he said. "Well, this is different."

In that moment—*whoa*—she wondered what she'd been thinking. *This is different?* What would he say next? *This is a big departure for you.* Or some other ridiculous thing.

But he didn't. He put his hands in his pockets and really looked at the paintings. Finally he said, "Have you shown them to Grimaldis?"

"Not yet. I haven't shown them to anyone."

"Are they done?"

"Do you think they're done?"

"They look just finished enough," he said. "I wouldn't do another thing to them. I would take photos down to Grimaldis and see what she says. She might give you a whole show."

Her heart uncrammed itself, just a little. She wondered if he was lying. But would he have come over at midnight just to tell her what he thought she wanted to hear? She had no idea. His cheating was too deep for her to comprehend. She wondered if she'd actually asked him over for an opinion or just to gauge his honesty. And then she wondered if she had called him over to have one last rush of sex with him.

He stood there looking beautiful and tired. He knew how he looked. He practiced this look. It was a very effective thing, like a perfect jacket he could put on and take off whenever he wanted.

She wondered if she really was that weak, that desperate, or that grateful for the favors he'd done for her out of what was, presumably, guilt. She felt angry that she depended so much on his opinion and that she was that out of touch with anyone else working at his level. Kelly, Marie, Justine, and Neary would all be appalled at just the consideration of sex with him, but the fact was, she *did* feel weak, desperate, and grateful. The apartment was, tritely, empty without him and these canvases of her own nude selves were thin company. When the world spun down to her shaved hair slowly growing back and the smell of paint at two in the morning, she had to admit, she was lonely and wouldn't mind helping him cheat, yet again, but this time with her, which, when she got right down to it, was probably what he was doing when they had first slept together. Maybe he was just one of those people for whom honesty was an odd appendage, useful when needed, and that was all. The only thing that kept her from doubting the things he'd said about her paintings was the fact that she felt the same way about them and that Grimaldis had liked her others.

She touched his arm anyway, his paint-stained fingers. "Thanks," she said, "thanks."

He looked surprised for a minute and then squeezed her hand. He obviously knew better than to say anything. She leaned over to kiss him, and he leaned into it with all the passion and victory she felt in herself at that very moment. She touched his chest and he ran his hand over what was left of her hair, bristly and just starting to grow back.

The Witch Bottle

You know it's irrational but you believe the nosy woman who lives next door is a witch.

Not the kind of witch who casts spells, but a poisoner. You know that there is such a thing because you've found it on the internet. You've found the antidote too; to avoid being poisoned by witches, take a blue bottle, fill it with your own fingernail clippings and hair, six metal nails and a little urine. Cork it and bury it upside down in the ground. That's what it says on the internet. You'll be safe from the most intimate sources of poison. The question of *why* she wants to poison you is a good one. Maybe you scared her cat when you pulled into the driveway. Maybe she was using those binoculars she keeps on the back porch, which she says are for watching birds, but didn't like what she saw when she was peeping through your blinds from her own house. Maybe she didn't like the way you make love to your wife, not that it's any of her business, not in any way at all, even if your wife isn't all that pleased with your sexual technique and puts up with it, and maybe said something to her girlfriends which may have somehow gotten back to the witch next door. Maybe the witch thinks she'd be doing your wife a favor by getting you out of the way.

The witch has a basement full of poisons and potions, if you listen to your kids. She lives alone and has no family to speak of. You tell your kids that it's nothing but a Halloween story that's gotten out of control, but deep in your heart, while you're looking around in the liquor store, you're keeping an eye out for something that comes in a blue bottle. You find two things: cheap Rieslings and a Bombay Blue Gin. You buy a couple of bottles of Riesling because you think you'll drink that faster than the gin. The wine is cheap enough that you could just pour it out and use the bottle right away. You wonder how you're going to explain the fingernail clippings, the hair and urine to your wife, much less the act of burying something in the back-yard. The backyard is a carefully landscaped postage stamp with-out a lot of room for a secret burial of a bottle or even a dead pet. When the dog died under suspicious circumstances last year you left the body at the vet's to be cremated, and now the dog sits in a solemn wooden box on the mantle over the gas fire-place. You blame the witch. You know you do.

You never talk about her if you can possibly help it. You think she might be a Lesbian, even though she never has any company, male or female. You've never trusted women who have no use for men. It makes you feel insecure, like a parasite on the back of her version of society. You would feel perfectly justified in poisoning her first before she could get to you.

Your wife and children are mostly oblivious to the witch next door and have never delved into the internet looking for preventions from poisoners but you fear for yourself and your family. The only one who you think might be safe is the family cat, which jumps the fence between your house and hers with-out hesitation and sits, sunning itself on her patio while the witch's cat watches jealously through a window.

You can't say exactly when you pinned her as a witch. Just a feeling about her as she puttered around in her own overgrown yard. It seems like she cultivates weeds. You've looked some of them up, like the burdock and lamb's ear, which seem harmless enough—even medicinal—but then there's the patio with the nightshade growing right out there in the open in its own pot. A sure sign of a poisoner?

At block parties, which happen twice a year, in the summer after school's out and in the fall just before Thanksgiving, she makes cookies, which, you have noticed, no one ever touches. It's tempting to ask the neighbors what they think. It's tempting to eat a cookie yourself—the hospital is only ten minutes from your house after all. How quickly could a nightshade cookie kill you? You have never seen her eat one of her own cookies, however, and so you never follow through on this impulse.

On Halloween, she dresses as a fairy and hands out Milky Ways, Snickers, 3 Musketeers, Hershey's Kisses and other pre-wrapped industrially produced candy so you don't worry about your kids eating *that*. What idiot witch would hand out poisoned candy on Halloween anyway, when everyone's on the lookout for razor blades in apples and glass shards? Besides, you are her target, not the neighborhood kids. You're certain of that.

One day, between Halloween and Thanksgiving, you run into her at the grocery store. You're buying milk, bread, toilet paper, and sanitary napkins. She takes a look at your cart and gives you a strange sort of smirk, like you're both stockpiling for a winter storm and at the same time you have a wussiness in you that allows you to be pushed around by your wife to get the most intimate products the store has to offer. She's smirking at your manliness and your unmanliness at the same time. You don't know what to say, even when she says "hello." You just push your cart past hers and pray you don't end up in the same checkout lane. How terribly awkward would that be? You pick up a steak and rush to pay and leave.

You don't see her again for days after that.

You work as a Project Manager for an engineering firm, which gives you flexible hours. You can work from home on certain days, which is nice. Your wife works as a shelf stocker at Wal-Mart so she's at work sometimes even on Saturdays and Sundays, which means you're either home alone or home with the kids after school. You do most of the cooking because of your wife's hours, which means you spend a lot of time looking through the kitchen window at the witch's doings next door. You've never seen her do anything like, say, draw a pentagram in chalk on her patio, or set out candles on the ground, but you just can't shake the feeling that she's out to get you and is simply biding her time until you let your guard down.

One morning when the kids are at school and your wife is out of the house, you call your mother and after a while you tell her your suspicions. You wouldn't mention them to anyone else, but your mother is superstitious and already tuned in to the fact that there's a lot of unexplainable shit going on in the world. She reads between the lines in the obituaries and has deep, abiding doubts about the Masons, but she's a good one to ask about the witch next door.

"Can she swim?" asks your mother. "In the old days they used to throw witches into a pond to see if they would float."

"People naturally float," you say. "What could that possibly prove?"

"What're you going to do if you *can* prove it?" asks your mother.

Your father, long dead, would disapprove of this conversation one hundred percent. He had been a very practical man—a professional plumber—and only just put up with his wife's hare-brained beliefs.

"I don't know," you say. "But if she tries to poison me, I could have her arrested."

"What you need are antidotes," says your mother and you tell her about the bottle, the difficulties you're having figuring out a place to bury it in the back.

"Just pick a spot," says your mother sounding exasperated. "Make sure she sees you digging the hole and putting it in. You can put in a rose bush on top if it bothers your wife so much. My God, how big a hole do you even need?"

"Not very big," you concede.

"Then just *do* it," says your mother, and she hangs up.

THE BOTTLE is already packed and stoppered. You've been keeping it under the bed where your wife won't find it. You take it down to the kitchen and peer out the window. Sure enough, the witch is sitting on her patio with your cat on her lap. You worry about the cat, but only for a moment. You go outside holding the blue wine bottle by the neck and get a shovel out of the small tool shed beside the back door. You glance sideways across the fence, which is only thigh-high. She has a good view of you and you have a good view of her. You go slowly to the back corner of the yard, set the bottle between yourself and her so it's in full view and begin to dig a hole. The ground is soft and yielding. Soon you're at bottle-depth, then a little deeper, then at about two feet. You stop and look over your shoulder. Your cat has jumped back into his yard and is coming over to see what you're doing. The witch has gotten out of her chair and is standing with her hands on her hips, watching too.

You turn the bottle over so it's pointing down, just like the instructions on the internet told you, ease the bottle into the hole and begin covering it with dirt. You wonder what the kids will do if they ever end up digging around out here. You finish covering the bottle and tamp down the dirt. The cat comes over and immediately pees where you've been digging, then scratches the dirt up in a pile to cover it. It's like a message. You turn to look at the witch.

She smiles at you in a *you're nuts* kind of way, waves and goes back into her house.

You, however, feel immediately better, proactive. Any evilness that has been cast in your direction will be trapped by this bottle. Better yet, it'll be deflected back at the witch, like a boomerang of ill-will. Though you've never really wished bad things on anyone, this is an exception. Being poisoned isn't something to take lightly. Not with a wife and family involved. Not when you're the main breadwinner and the kids aren't even in middle school yet.

You brush off your hands, put the shovel away and go back into the house to get some work done before noon.

After lunch, you pause by the kitchen window to find the witch's cat digging in the freshly turned earth. Under any other circumstances it would be a strictly territorial thing between cats. Now it's between you and the witch. You storm outside and shoo the cat, which is black with white paws, away. You turn to see the witch standing on her patio to receive her—let's just call it what it is—her familiar.

"Hey," you call across the yard. "Keep your cat on your side of the fence!"

"Then keep yours on your side," she shouts back.

Stalemate, you think. Cats will go wherever they feel like going unless they're locked inside. Still, you feel you have the advantage in this situation. The bottle is too deeply buried for a cat. The only way for her to really get to it is to sneak over in the middle of the night and dig it out herself, in which case you'll just call the police and have her arrested for trespassing. But first you have to catch her at it. You glance over at the little patch of ground and think about staying up all night to guard it. How would you even know if she'd been over to dig it up otherwise? Would a motion detector and some sort of alarm be justified? That would mean a trip to the hardware store, which you don't have time for. You're already behind on this project and tomorrow you actually have to go into the office, which means the bottle will be unguarded. You wonder if you should get a guard dog, but this seems like excessive thinking, beyond even what your mother would consider reasonable. You go back upstairs to work on the damn project and can hardly keep your mind on it. When the kids come home from school, you're in a terrible mood. When your wife comes home, dinner still isn't ready and you feel like tearing your hair out.

You wonder if it's not poisoning you have to worry about after all but some kind of spell. You wish you could talk to your wife about this, but she would look at you like you were out of your mind and frankly, you're beginning to have doubts about yourself as well.

You go to bed that night, exhausted, but barely sleep. You go down to the kitchen three times and turn on the outside light to see if anything is going on in the yard. Each time, nothing. The patch of dirt is undisturbed. Sometime around two in the morning, you fall deeply asleep. At five, your alarm crashes into your dreams about peeing into the bottle. You wake up, get your shit together and go to work before anyone else even gets out of bed.

DURING A STAFF MEETING, it occurs to you that you've only managed to curse yourself with the damn bottle and that the witch next door didn't have to lift a finger to make your life miserable. You wonder whether to dig it up under cover of darkness and bury it somewhere else. You get on the internet while the meeting is still going on. You find archaeological evidence of witch bottles being hidden under hearth stones or thresholds, or even plastered into the walls of houses. You decide these are impractical solutions. There's a basement under the gas fireplace, not a dirt foundation. The threshold, such as it is, is covered with a concrete porch. The walls are drywall and punching a hole in one to deposit the bottle would only raise questions you really don't want to answer. You wish you could just forget about it. Someone in the meeting is asking you something. You answer as best you can. You feel cursed by how stupid you sound. At the moment, you can totally understand how someone might want to burn a witch, just to get her permanently out of your life.

When you get home you check the place where the bottle is buried. No one has touched it, as far as you can tell. The kids want to know why you dug in the backyard when they're not allowed to and you tell them you were planting some new kind of flower. They want to plant flowers, too. You forbid them, then send them out front to ride their tricycles in the driveway.

The witch is out tending her weeds. Some of the weeds have flowers, like the black-eyed susans and the phlox. Some of it is pretty, but you don't want to get sucked into admiring her yard, especially when it's so overgrown compared to yours. You have the corner lot, so there is no neighbor on the other side of you, only on the other side of her yard and those people never complain, not even during the block parties. They're patently oblivious, you've decided. You're the only one who really knows what's going on. You realize you're ready to break into her house to find out if the kids are right about what she has in the basement. You try, very hard, not to dwell on this idea.

One Saturday when everyone is home, the witch knocks on the door to borrow a cup of sugar. Your wife, as oblivious as the rest of the neighborhood, cheerfully goes off to the kitchen to get some. You're in the living room on your laptop with a direct view of the front door where the witch is waiting. The kids, who are too young to know better, come right up to her and ask her if she makes magic potions in her basement. The witch laughs and asks where they got such silly ideas and they both turn and point at you. You feel the heat rise in your face and close the laptop.

"I never said that," you say. "They came up with that idea themselves."

The witch only shrugs. "You're the one burying bottles in the backyard."

Your wife, back from the kitchen with a measuring cup full of sugar, stops and gives you an odd look.

"I never buried anything," you lie. "The cat's been scratching up the dirt back there. I planted some seeds, that's all."

"What're you baking?" your wife asks the witch conversationally.

"Cookies," says the witch in a tone that sounds ominous, at least to you. "I'll bring over a batch when I'm done."

You immediately decide to forbid the children to eat them and to secretly throw them away.

"Thanks," says your wife, and closes the door. She turns to you with a faintly accusing expression but doesn't say anything, and goes back to the kitchen where you can hear her noisily start to do the dishes. She has to leave for work in an hour, which means you will be the one fixing dinner, staring out your kitchen window into the witch's, watching the cookies come out of the oven, just like some Hansel and Gretel nightmare scenario. You wonder if there's a place you could get the cookies tested for poisons and can't think of anything. A poison control hotline would be something to use after the fact, and then it would be too late. Besides, they would ask what your child had ingested and what would you be able to tell them? Sugar and nightshade? You are dreading the witch's second visit, tonight, with cookies. How will you keep the kids out of them? Maybe best not to be home at all. You decide to take the kids to McDonald's and a movie tonight. You have a ton of things to do, but avoiding these cookies would be worth the time. You can imagine coming home to a prettily-wrapped gift basket on your front stairs, whisking it away and telling the kids it's too late to have any sugar. You feel better knowing you've solved the problem by using avoidance rather than confrontation. You open the laptop again and get back to work until your wife has to leave.

THE KIDS are thrilled to be going out for junk food and a movie, which is both loud and juvenile. It's a Saturday, so at least it's not a school night because you get back pretty late. Sure enough, there's a basket with cookies on the front steps. You tell the kids exactly what you've rehearsed in your mind, and they grumpily brush their teeth and go to bed. Your wife is due home at eleven. You put the cookies down the garbage disposal except for one, which you sniff at and break into pieces. It looks, smells and feels exactly like a freshly made chocolate chip cookie. You take your life into your hands and taste it with the tip of your tongue. After all, the bottle is buried in the backyard. Aren't you protected? The cookie tastes perfectly ordinary. You feel a momentary stab of regret at putting all those cookies down the drain. What if this was a peace offering? But no. You can't get yourself to quite believe that. The cookies are a trick, a trap. You dispose of the final cookie and peer out the kitchen window. The witch's house is completely dark. Maybe she, too, went out for dinner and a movie, or maybe she just went to bed early. In any case, not sure what else to do, you call your mother again and tell her what's going on.

"You have to get into her house," says your mother with absolute certainty. "You'll never know what's really going on over there until you see the basement."

"But what about the backyard?" you say. "What about the nightshade in the planter? Isn't that proof enough?"

"I'm not saying break in and rob her," says your mother indignantly. "I'm just saying maybe she's not much of a yard person. Frankly, you're a little obsessive about yours. Maybe it just looks like a weed-patch from your point of view. My point is, if you think she's got a poison lab in there, you need to see it with your own eyes. That's all."

Your wife won't be home for another hour. You hang up and stand in the kitchen of the silent house and make up your mind to go next door. You put on your coat and stand at your own front door for a long moment making sure you really want to do this before you step outside.

YOU WALK OVER the grassy strip that separates your house from hers and up her front steps. You knock timidly at the front door, knowing that no one is home and that even if she were, she wouldn't be able to hear you.

After another long moment, you try the doorknob.

To your surprise, the knob turns and the door opens.

This tells you two important things: A) the witch is too trusting of this neighborhood. *You* would never leave your front door unlocked. B) this is a trap and the witch is waiting for you to come on in and be caught in the act of a home invasion. She could easily call the police on you, long before you could get to the basement and check things out. For once you wonder why you ever listen to your mother.

The door swings ever wider, like an invitation.

You take a breath. "Hello?" you call into the house. There is no answer. Just darkness. There are two things you could do right now: A) shut the door, go home and forever wonder what you might have found if you'd had the balls to go into a dark house where a witch lives, or B) get the hell in there, look around and then get the hell out.

You choose option B.

All the houses in your neighborhood are built on exactly the same floor plan, so finding the basement door is no challenge, even in total blackness, but you don't want to navigate the stairs in the dark so you reach for the light and holding your breath, turn it on. Nothing happens. Nothing moves. No sound at all.

You go down the stairs, which are carpeted and silent.

At the bottom, the carpeting comes to an end and you see it. The plank benches with bubbling fluids in containers that look like they came from a chemistry set. The smell hits you. Cat litter mixed with something that sticks at the top of your throat, cloying and sweet. You can just see the hanks of dried plants hanging from clothesline strung along the ceiling. You stand there, transfixed, not believing that you were really right about her being a witch in this day and age until you realize that you are being watched. You look slowly to your right, into the dark of the room and see two reflective eyes staring right at you.

You let out a squeak of fear and race back up the steps. You're out her front door and back at your own when you realize that it was probably the cat in the basement, and worse, the cat probably recognized you and will tell the witch exactly what went on while she wasn't there. You know these thoughts are irrational. You're already trying to rationalize what you saw—maybe she's an herbalist, or an amateur chemist. Maybe she's making artisanal beer—or even crystal meth—but deep in your gut you know that she's a witch and that you have put yourself and your family at great risk just now by going into her house. Who but the most confident minion of the devil would leave a house like that unlocked in the middle of the night?

You try to remember if you turned off her basement light and are pretty sure you did.

You get the second bottle of Riesling, empty it into the toilet, piss into it, clip your nails and trim your hair and put it all in there together with a couple of metal hairpins, just to be safe and stuff the cork back in. You get the shovel out of the shed and are digging another hole in the garden when your wife gets home fifteen minutes later.

"Don't ask questions," you tell her, panting, when she finds you out there, tamping down earth on the other side of the yard from the first bottle. You're wondering if putting a bottle at each corner of the yard is a good idea or if two is enough.

"What the hell are you doing?" she demands. "Don't you remember how much we spent landscaping this place?"

"That's not the point," you say, and try to tell her, without actually telling her that you were just in the next door neighbor's basement snooping around, that she and the entire family may be in grave danger.

"What do you mean 'grave danger'?" she demands again. "What the hell is going on around here?"

You finally have to admit you were in the witch's basement and tell her what you saw.

"She has a chemistry set down there?" says your wife. "But you think she's making poisoned cookies?"

You tell her about the nightshade and everything else that's made you suspect that the neighbor is a dangerous supernatural being—leaving out any mention of your mother, however—and your wife just laughs at you.

"Well anyway," you say, "nothing's wrong with burying a few things in the yard, just to make sure." And then she makes you describe what you're burying and laughs even harder, reminding you of which century it is, scoffing at all the silly superstitions you've piled up over the last months, scoffing at your internet finds, and the internet in general and its supposed knowledge. Rather than spend any more time out in the dark with you and your shovel and your buried bottles, your wife goes inside to make herself some dinner and turn on the TV. You get the impression she's about done with you and the crazy shit you sometimes find yourself in. This adds to your level of anxiety, because perhaps instead of poison, the witch is casting spells to break the two of you up. You try to make yourself feel how ridiculous this actually sounds, but your mind is already on this track and it's hard to get off. You look over at the witch's house and see a single light on upstairs, as though she's come home and gone upstairs to bed. You wonder if she's been watching you bury the second bottle. Futility washes over you. If she knows about the bottles, maybe you're not safe after all. Maybe secrecy was the way to go. Midnight burials and inverted pentagrams. On the other hand, maybe she's not a witch after all, but just a common kook, which is why the bottles aren't working. But you're the one who walked into her house. Maybe *you're* the common kook. You feel like your wife is right about everything and you drop the shovel where it is and go into the house to apologize to her and perhaps offer to seek professional help, to be a better lover—but none of this means you *didn't* find the poison factory in her basement. You open the back door and decide the way to solve this whole thing is to call the police. It would be hard to incriminate you of anything. After all, the only one who saw you in the basement was the witch's cat, and it's unlikely that cat's evidence will be taken in a police report. You regret, now, disposing of the cookies.

You go in with the phone in your hand and tell your wife what you intend to do. She rolls her eyes and holds out her hand for the phone.

"It's ten o'clock at night," she says. "We're not calling the police to do a witch hunt at this hour."

"When?" you say. "Tomorrow? I know what I saw."

"Tomorrow," says your wife, "I'll go over there and invite myself in for tea or something and I'll make her give me the tour of her house. And the yard. We'll see what she's growing out there. Who knows? Maybe she's making herbal essences in her basement. You saw dried plants hanging from the ceiling?" You nod and so does your wife, but dismissively. "We'll just see what's really going on over there."

"She's not going to *tell* you she's concocting poisons," you say.

"Of course not," says your wife, "but I'll be able to tell if something fishy's going on. Then we'll see about calling the police."

THAT NIGHT you hardly sleep. You get up and do some of the work you've been putting off. From the room you use as an office you can see the light from the witch's downstairs windows casting a glow over her overgrown garden and you know she's up too, possibly dismantling her basement lab. You look at the clock. It's about three. Even if you called the police right now, they'd accuse you of dreaming. Your wife is right about waiting for the light of day, but by morning there may be nothing left to see.

IN THE MORNING you fix pancakes for everybody, but especially for your wife as a sort of apology for all your crazy behavior. In return, as soon as she's done, she dabs her lips with a napkin and announces that she's going next door for a visit. You find that you desperately want to go too, but you hold yourself back and do the dishes instead. From the kitchen window you see the witch go to answer the door when your wife rings the bell. You realize you should have told her about the cookies so there would at least be an icebreaker—*thanks for the cookies—so neighborly*—but too late for that now. As you stand there, scrubbing syrup off the kids' plates, you wonder again what the witch has against you and think, that perhaps, everything boils down to what you have against the witch. You see the witch making tea on the stovetop and wonder if you should be fearing for your wife's safety. But that would be ridiculous, right? Because there's no such thing as a witch and your wife is over there being the adult in this situation, not the juvenile house-breaker, like you.

You watch your wife take the teacup but not drink any of it. You see them sit down at the kitchen counter and have a good laugh over something, silent-movie-like, and probably you. The cat jumps up on the table. The witch strokes its head and then the two of them get up and move out of sight. You stay right where you are, scrubbing, rinsing, and drying, waiting for something to happen.

You wait a good half hour and no one comes back into view. All you can see are the two teacups cooling on the kitchen counter. How the hell long does it take to get a tour of a house anyway? You could take a visitor through yours in less than fifteen minutes and that would include exploring the closets. In the background noise behind you, the kids are watching Barney on TV. It's nerve-racking. You squeeze out the dishrag like you were wringing a neck. It's almost time to go over there yourself. You make yourself wait another ten minutes, make it another five, and when the clock reads 8:20, you dry off your hands and admonish the kids to be good while you go next door. The kids do not care where you go or when you get back. They still remember the cookies and hold that against you.

You hurry over to the witch's front door and ring the bell and knock for good measure. You think about trying the knob, which you're pretty sure is unlocked. You're pretty sure you could walk right in, but you really don't want to this time. You really want your wife to appear at the door with a puzzled but incriminating expression on her face, and then you want to call the cops.

The door opens and it's the witch. Your wife is nowhere in sight. The witch gives you that same *you're nuts* look and ushers you inside. Your wife appears from the kitchen with a victorious look on her face which you can't exactly decipher, but you suspect means the worst for you. No doubt the basement has been transformed into something totally ordinary, like a home gym, or a hobby room full of knickknacks and sewing projects.

"I was just wondering when you'd be getting home," you say. "We were going to the grocery store this morning," or some such horseshit. You just want her out of this house.

"Coming," says your wife, ever so sweetly and she holds up a ziplock bag of chocolate chip cookies. "Thank you so much," she says to the witch. "So thoughtful of you. So neighborly."

"You're welcome," says the witch, "stop by any time."

BACK AT YOUR OWN HOUSE, you grill your wife in a part of the house where the kids can't hear you. "Well?" you say, *"Well?"*

Your wife brandishes the cookies. "You're right," she says, "she has some kind of lab down there. She says she makes herbal soaps, but I didn't see any soap, just liquid stuff and these—" the incriminating cookies.

"So!" you crow. "You think I was right!"

"No," says your wife, "I don't think she's a witch but I do think she's some kind of nut and I wouldn't let the kids near these things."

"So we should call the cops."

"Go get the phone," says your wife. "I'll make the call myself."

LONG STORY SHORT, the police show up, full of skepticism, but when they examine the cookies, one of them offers to have them tested for an array of known poisons. They take the cookies and all of your information and you tell them everything except for the part where you filled two blue bottles full of pee and fingernails and of course the part where you broke into the witch's house. When the cops walk out of your house with the bag of cookies you realize the witch is watching all of this. You feel a momentary pang for her, but it doesn't last very long, because you're pretty damn sure the cookies are poisoned.

THE NEXT DAY there's a for sale sign pounded into the witch's front yard. You look up the price on the internet and find out how low she's willing to go for a quick sale. To you and your wife it's an admission of guilt, plus an enormous relief.

Even before the cops come back with a report on the cookies, the witch has moved out. You see her once, supervising the movers but she doesn't look at you. She studiously ignores you. As they pass through the door and into the moving van, you search her belongings for any sign of the poison-lab set in the basement but if it's still around, it's packed away in boxes.

After she leaves, her weedy yard goes further to seed, looking worse and worse. Still, for the right price, even a weedchoked single-family home will sell and within a month there are new neighbors next door. Normal people with a colicky baby and a dog that barks incessantly.

The cops come back with a report that the cookies were fine and in fact delicious, and you really don't know how to feel.

Deep inside you have no doubts about what she was, but instead of a satisfying feeling of accomplishment, you feel the slightest twinges of guilt. You fight those off, especially at three in the morning. After all, haven't you defended the neighborhood from the forces of evil?

You know what you saw. You know what you know. You were right and just to prove it, you let your wife watch you bury two more bottles in the remaining corners of the yard.

The Stages

HEATHER WOKE UP in the bright room.

Everything was familiar. She'd woken up here in Recovery a year ago after a double mastectomy. Now it was her womb that was gone, and with it, with any luck, all of the cancer.

The nurse, in green scrubs, with white streaks in her black hair, adjusted Heather's IV. "You awake, honey?" she said.

Heather moved her lips dryly.

"Good," said the nurse. "We'll have you up in your room in about half an hour. Your family's waiting for you."

Her husband, Jack and her daughter, Gina. Jack, who was withdrawing as the doctors removed bits of her, piece by piece. Gina, who would be sixteen tomorrow, clinging to what was left.

"Do you know...?" Heather whispered to the nurse. "Do you know if they got it all?"

"Doctor Asumadu will have your pathology report this afternoon. Okay? Do you want some ice chips?"

Heather nodded and the nurse disappeared. Heather closed her eyes. When she opened them, the room had changed. There was a window with a cloud in a blue March sky. Gina was on her right saying, "Mom, are you thirsty? Mom?"

Gina had come to the hospital with Jack and was missing

a day of school. The surgery had been at seven. What time was it now? Heather looked around for a clock, but all she could see was her daughter, blonde hair combed out straight, down to her shoulders. Her face, which looked so much like a young Jack, with her optimistic eyebrows and high cheekbones—that all-American look. In their early days, Heather had teased Jack that he could've been a model, a movie star instead of just a handsome engineer. Now her daughter's good looks just seemed to be a handicap. Good looks and lousy grades.

"Mom!" Gina was sitting on the edge of the bed now. "Ice chips!"

Heather opened her mouth and let Gina put an ice chip on her tongue. It was cold and wet and she was very thirsty. She let it melt and swallowed.

"Is there water?" she whispered.

"I'll get you some." Gina got off the bed and took a blue plastic cup to the bathroom.

"How're you feeling?" said Jack, standing with his arms crossed.

She was pretty sure he didn't care. Over the years she had discovered that he was a beautiful but simple creature. What was left for him now that her womanhood was gone? Her mind? He had never taken that part of her seriously. She was only a teacher. For little kids. How hard could that be? So she had two degrees. He had three. It was always some kind of competition with him.

"I'm okay."

"Good," he said.

In the last year he hadn't touched her, except by accident,

bumping into her in the kitchen, one arm flung across her when he was asleep. Once her breasts were gone, he'd lost interest. She'd opted out of reconstructive surgery because of the way he'd been. New breasts weren't going to be as good as the old ones. He'd liked feasting on the old ones until they got lumpy and she got scared. After the mastectomy, the chemo, the radiation, he was just impatient. Heather suspected that he was having an affair with someone younger and more complete. Someone who didn't give a shit about his family.

Gina came back with the water and sat on the edge of the bed. She watched as Heather sipped. Was it normal, Heather wondered, for a teenaged girl to be so protective and thoughtful of her mother? Weren't they breaking away at this point, learning to drive, staying out late, and ignoring the adults in their lives? Heather had friends who taught high school and friends with teenaged kids. Instead of rolling their eyes at Gina's behavior, they looked at her as though something crucial was missing. Rebellion. Where was it in her daughter? Had it evaporated in a puff under this kind of pressure? Was she going to be one of those children who turned into a diamond after being crushed by misery? And the other question—would she, Heather, live long enough to find out?

Heather gave Gina the blue plastic cup and eased down in the bed. Under the sheet and blanket and flimsy hospital robe was a new scar, horizontal, inches below her navel. In a month maybe, it would match the scars where her breasts had been, forming a scratchily-drawn face on the front of her body. Two flat eyes and a straight-across mouth. It was the same expression she saw on herself when she looked in the mirror these days. It was the holding-back-panic look, especially when Doctor Asumadu had probed her belly with his warm fingers and ordered an MRI. These things often happen together, he'd said. Breast cancer and uterine cancer.

She closed her eyes. She wasn't a religious person. Neither was Jack, and to the best of her knowledge, neither was Gina, but somewhere in the center of her stomach was the urge to pray. To anybody or anything. To make this all be over.

"Mom," said Gina, "the doctor's here."

Had she fallen asleep? Suddenly Doctor Asumadu was standing by the bed. There was a clock behind him and somehow it was three in the afternoon.

"How are you feeling, Mrs. North?" he asked in his soft, Ghanaian accent.

"I don't know," said Heather, feeling woozy and not really present.

"Are you in any pain?" He eyed the morphine drip. He was tall, like Jack, and she felt like she was looking up at his face from a tremendous distance.

"I don't think so."

"Good," he said. "You'll tell the nurse immediately if we need to increase your pain medication." He gestured to his right and a nurse materialized, this time a black woman in pink scrubs, smiling. "I have your pathology report," said Doctor Asumadu.

"What's it say?" said Gina, off to the right. Heather looked over as Gina's hand slid into hers. Gina's palm was warm and sweaty. Gina's face looked pale. Jack was standing behind her, holding a Styrofoam coffee cup.

"I'm afraid the news is not good," said Doctor Asumadu.

"As we suspected when we did the MRI, we found your uterus to be completely compromised by the cancer. Unfortunately, it did not stop there, and has spread beyond where we could safely remove it. I'm afraid your cancer has metastasized, and your lymph system has been affected as well."

Heather swallowed in a dry mouth and squeezed Gina's hand, hard.

"So," said Jack, "that means more chemo and radiation."

"Chemo, yes," said Doctor Asumadu. "I recommend an aggressive course. But given the rate that the cancer has progressed in such a short time, treatment will give you approximately six months to live, Mrs. North," he said, looking down at Heather. "I'm sorry to be the bearer of such bad news, but it is time to get your affairs in order."

"Oh," whispered Heather. "I see."

"*I* don't see," snapped Gina. "*I* thought she was going to be all right after this was over."

"Unfortunately," said Doctor Asumadu, "there was no way to tell how serious and widespread the cancer was from looking at the MRI. We tried to be preemptive. But we were not soon enough."

He spoke to Gina as though she were an adult, which Heather appreciated. She would've been infuriated if he had spoken down to her child. Infuriated. Was that how she should feel anyway? He had said she was going to die. That hadn't come up in her conversations with him before, only in her searches on the internet—which she had dismissed as paranoid.

"Why didn't you tell me this before?" she said to him, looking up through the long distance to his gentle brown eyes.

"I thought," he said, and he sounded sad and defeated, "that we had caught it. I was wrong. And I'm very sorry."

The nurse in pink scrubs was no longer smiling.

Jack said, "I'm going to sue your ass for medical malpractice."

"You may certainly try," said Doctor Asumadu. "Please feel free to contact the hospital's legal department." He looked down at Heather again. "Do you have any questions, Mrs. North?"

"Six months?" she whispered, and he nodded. "Will it hurt?"

"We will make sure you have medication for pain," he said.

"When can she go home?" said Gina.

"In two days," said Doctor Asumadu. There was a long silence, and after a while, he said, "Do you have any questions, Mr. North?"

Jack just shook his head.

ON MONDAY, when Heather was discharged, Jack showed up and fidgeted with the wheelchair she was supposed to get into. Doctor Asumadu came with papers for her to sign and wound-care instructions. He also gave her a container of Percocet.

"You will take these every six hours for two weeks," he said. "You will call me if you feel uncomfortable and I will increase the dosage. All right?"

The Percocet would knock her out. She'd had it before, after the mastectomy. Two weeks of her life would escape, like air from a balloon. What fraction of six months was two weeks? This was something she taught the little kids at school, but now it was beyond her. Should she ask Jack? She was too weary to figure it out herself. "All right."

"Make an appointment with my nurse," said Doctor Asumadu. "In two weeks I will remove your stitches."

He didn't say what he'd said after her mastectomy, which was, "and then you can return to your normal activities."

JACK WHEELED HER down to the elevator, past the gift shop and through the modern, airy lobby, without saying anything.

At the front door, he set the brake on the wheelchair. "I'll get the car."

She watched him go, tall and tense, dressed in jeans and a grey sweater. Was it a work day? She'd lost track. Was Gina in school? Hopefully. Right. It was Monday. She rolled the pill bottle between her fingers and wondered about taking a Percocet now, so as to fall asleep on the ride home and not have to talk about anything for forty-five minutes. She looked up at the circular drive, watching for Jack's red Toyota, and noticed, for the first time, the people around her, also waiting, or shuffling, or walking towards the hospital with concerned expressions on their faces. How many of these people were dying, she wondered, or was she the only one?

JACK DIDN'T SAY MUCH on the way home. Only, "You want to listen to music?" and turned the radio to a Sirius station that played soft Jazz, called *Intimacy.* Heather could picture Jack and some other woman in the car, listening to *Intimacy.* She wished she'd taken the Percocet.

"What're we going to do about Gina?" she said finally, about halfway home.

"Well," said Jack. "In two years she'll be in college. Between what we have in savings and your, um, benefits, we'll be able to cover half her tuition. She'll have to get a job for the rest."

Jesus Christ. "I'm not talking about college," said Heather. "Or anything like that. I was talking about her birthday."

"Oh," said Jack. "Oh yeah. Sorry. I just thought you meant...well. What do you want to do for her?"

"Does she want a party?" said Heather. "Should we get her friends together and, you know, pretend things are normal?"

"I don't like her friends," said Jack. "They're all pierced and tattooed. Anyway, they don't seem like party people."

"Have you met them?" said Heather, even though she knew he hadn't. She hadn't really, either. The friends—and they were uniformly pierced and tattooed—waited in their car for Gina to take her to school in the morning. When she didn't go, Heather was the one who answered the door, usually in her bathrobe. At the door was one of two different boys, possibly brothers. They both had stringy black hair, blue-inked Gothic lettering around their necks that she couldn't quite read, and tattered clothing. If she had to guess, she would've said they were seventeen-ish. If pressed, she would've said they were repeating a grade. Whichever one it was at the door, he would stare at his shoes and ask if Gina was coming today. It broke Heather's heart to think that her daughter was having sex with one, or possibly both of them. She wondered if Jack had thought about that and bet that he had. She wondered if he felt as powerless to stop the awful momentum of their daughter's life.

"What are we going to do about Gina?" she said, talking about the future now.

"What do you mean?" he said, more careful this time.

"I mean college. You and I both know her grades aren't good enough to get her into anything but community college."

"Then let her go," said Jack. "She can get an associate's degree in something useful. Like...an X-ray tech, or whatever."

"You could help her, you know," said Heather. "With her math, her science. The only thing she gets decent grades in is English, and that's only when they do a poetry unit."

"I don't know how to help her," said Jack, and he actually sounded sad. "Anyway, she doesn't want my help."

"So, what you *mean*," said Heather angrily, "is that you've already given up on her. Just like you've given up on me."

"Honey, I haven't given up on you—"

"You *have*," she said savagely. "You think I don't know you're sleeping with someone else. But I *do*."

He didn't say anything. He turned up the music and didn't say a word.

HOME WAS a split-level in the wooded suburbs. Gina wasn't back from school yet, even though it was three-thirty and school had ended an hour ago. Heather didn't say anything to Jack, just went to their bedroom upstairs, took a Percocet and lay down in her clothes, waiting for it to hit. After three days in the hospital, it was good to be home, to see the same familiar flat white ceiling. Her silence would be an unspoken command for Jack to sleep on the couch tonight. She would have the king bed to herself. She could flail around in her sleep, or stay as still as a, well, as a corpse when the Percocet took over. She was sorry she'd taken the pill for a minute. She'd sleep through Gina coming home. She'd sleep through whatever percentage of her life this was turning out to be. The haze of the drug crept over her. Heather closed her eyes, and slowly, with an effort, pushed her shoes off with her toes.

GINA WOKE her for dinner. "I fixed spaghetti and meatballs," she said. It was the only thing she knew how to cook. "Get up. It's getting cold."

THE DINING ROOM looked out on the neighbor's backyard, where there was fresh mulch and green things growing up through it. Their own yard, in comparison, was yellowish winter grass, with dead weeds around the edges. Somewhere out there was a little patch of ground where Heather had put in a vegetable garden last summer. The tomatoes had done well, but the lettuce had bolted, and no one would eat the broccoli, no matter how Heather fixed it. Nobody in the house liked broccoli—she wasn't even sure why she'd planted it. It was interesting to watch how it grew out, though, the petite yellow flowers blooming above the green heads, making it completely inedible, but pretty nonetheless.

Heather cut a meatball in half with her fork and wound up a spool of spaghetti. She almost had it in her mouth when Gina started talking.

"So," she said, "like. I have an announcement to make."

Heather put down her food. Jack, at the other end of the table, looked up as though he'd only just noticed that Gina was there.

"What is it, honey?" said Heather.

"Well, it's kind of a big deal." Gina licked her lips and Heather felt her stomach drop. "Danny and I, are, uh, gonna get married."

"Danny?" said Jack.

"Danny?" echoed Heather.

"He's the one you don't like," said Gina. "With the neck tats and the nose ring."

"But there's two of them," said Heather. "Which one's Danny? And what do you mean, you're getting married? You're way too young for that."

Gina rolled her eyes. Here was the rebellion, Heather thought. Like a bomb going off. Here it was at last. "There's Danny and Mike. Danny's taking welding. He's got a job already and he's eighteen. Mike's the one with the lip stud?" She brushed her mouth, head cocked. "And, I'm *not* too young."

"Oh my God," said Heather. "Are you pregnant?"

Gina flushed from her neck to her scalp. She didn't need to say anything.

"Oh my God," said Heather, "How could you let this happen? Didn't I teach you about birth control in middle school?"

"I didn't just 'let it happen,'" said Gina. "I did it on purpose. I did it for you, Mom."

"What?" said Heather, at the same time Jack said, "You're getting an abortion," in the same tone as he'd said, "I'm suing you for medical malpractice."

Gina turned to him. "Fuck you, Dad," she said. "Mom's going to have a grandchild. If you don't want it, then—then fuck you."

"Watch. Your. Mouth," said Jack, white-hot.

"That is *not*," Heather said to Gina, "something you have to do for me."

"It *is*," said Gina. "Because all you've got is a cheating husband and a loser kid. And you're going to stay alive for this, because—because I'm already at three months."

Heather swallowed hard. "What on earth made you think I wanted a grandchild?"

Gina narrowed her eyes. "Everyone wants one. Danny's mom is *thrilled*. I thought you would be, too," she said sullenly.

"What about Danny's father?" said Jack. "Is he *thrilled?*"

"Danny's dad left when he was four," said Gina. "Nobody cares what he thinks."

"You know," said Jack, "boys who grow up without fathers tend to do exactly what their own fathers did."

"You mean, like, leave me?" Gina turned on him savagely. "The way you're going to leave mom for your bitch-whore? Just when she really fucking needs you?" Tears spilled down her face. "Or were you going to wait for Mom to die, and then leave *me?*"

"No one's going to leave you," said Jack, pale now, his five o'clock shadow making his face a sort of ghastly blue. "I'm not going to. And I don't have a—I mean, I would *never...*"

"You're such a fucking *liar!*" Gina shouted over her half-eaten spaghetti. She shoved her chair away from the table and got up. "I'm only *sixteen!* What else am I supposed to *do?*" She stormed out of the dining room. In a minute Heather could hear her storming up the stairs to her bedroom. In a minute, the door slammed.

Heather rubbed her temples, blurry from the drugs. "Guess she's got you pegged."

"You've poisoned her mind," Jack snapped back.

"Oh," said Heather. "This is my fault? She's afraid *you're* going to abandon her."

"Well, I'm not," said Jack hotly. "Neither one of you. So you can stop worrying." He pushed his chair back. "She's not marrying that kid."

"Over my dead body, right?" said Heather and smiled when he looked horrified.

JACK SLEPT on the couch that night, and as far as Heather was concerned that was where he could stay until the day she died. She lay in the big bed by herself, trying to remember the stages of grief, or the stages of accepting death, and couldn't. There was Denial and Anger, but the Percocet prevented her from putting the stages in the right order. All she could recall was a scene from some musical where the main character, dying, shouted *I accept!!* and then what happened? Did he die? Was he saved by some miracle? She couldn't remember. If only she could think of the title, she could watch it again, and relearn all the stuff that seemed to be important now.

She woke up to the sound of Gina puking in the bathroom down the hall. The clock by the bed said it was six in the morning. The drugs had worn off and Heather could feel each stitch in her belly. She listened to her daughter vomiting and felt her own nausea at the sound. The combination of pain and sickness was unbearable. She pushed herself out of the bed and hobbled down the hall, to where Gina was kneeling in front of the toilet, her hair unbrushed, pushed back behind her ears.

"Are you okay?" said Heather, hand to Gina's forehead.

Gina leaned heavily into her hand and wiped her mouth with toilet paper. She flushed, but the smell of puke lingered. "I'm okay," she whispered and spat into the bowl.

"Rinse your mouth out," said Heather. "You'll feel better."

Gina did that. Heather reached into the medicine cabinet and found the Percocet. When Gina was done with the sink, she scooped up a handful of water and swallowed one down.

"Aren't you supposed to take those with food?" said Gina hoarsely.

"Is there food?" said Heather. "Did your father go shopping while I was in the hospital?"

"There's cereal," said Gina. "I think the milk's still good."

"Do you want to eat?" said Heather, and Gina shook her head.

"It's okay," said Gina. "I'll sit with you. I'll make some tea."

Downstairs they sat together at the dining table. The kitchen sink was full of spaghetti sauce-encrusted dishes. Jack was nowhere to be seen. Heather thought dully that he had either gone to work very early or had spent the night...somewhere else.

"Where's your dad?" she said, but Gina just shrugged, dipping her teabag in the steaming hot water. "Are you going to school today?" said Heather.

"I guess," said Gina. "I mean, I should. Danny says I missed a test in English. But if you need me to stay home, I will."

"No," said Heather. "You should go. I'll be fine."

"I'll take a shower," said Gina, and left her tea, with the bag still in it, cooling on the table.

Heather slowly got herself a bowl of Cheerios. If today was like any other day, Danny would be here to pick Gina up in about forty-five minutes. Heather would ask him to come in this time. They would have a little talk over cups of tea. If Danny drank tea. For all she knew he drank soda for breakfast. She wondered if there was any soda in the house. Whatever their conversation veered toward, it would have to veer quickly. The drugs were hitting, and hitting hard. She spooned Cheerios into her mouth methodically, not because she could actually taste them, but because she knew she had to eat to stay alive, at least for a little while.

Gina came downstairs, dressed and drying her hair. She was wearing old jeans, stylishly torn at the knees, and a white midriff-baring T-shirt. *Wear it while you can*, thought Heather. *In a month you won't fit into those pants.*

"Feeling better?" she said.

"Yeah." Gina slurped her cold tea and glanced at the clock. She poured herself a bowl of cereal, sat and ate it dry, with her fingers.

"Don't you want any milk?" said Heather, rather hopelessly. She had wanted marshmallows and Pepsi when she'd been pregnant with this child.

Gina shook her head. "I really want spaghetti," she said, "but Dad threw it all out."

Heather took a steadying breath. "We're going to have to talk soon," she said. "About babies. Things you'll need to know. We'll need to get you to a prenatal exam. Find an obstetrician you like. Danny should go with you to your appointments."

"I don't know if he'll be able to," said Gina, crunching Cheerios. "Between school and work. I don't know. Besides, it was my decision. It's my responsibility."

"It's his responsibility too," said Heather.

"I know," said Gina, not looking up. "But I was the one who decided not to use condoms that time."

"Wait a minute," said Heather. "This wasn't his idea, too?"

"Sure it was."

"Are you telling me," said Heather slowly, feeling thick in the head, like this might be a terrible hallucination, "that he hasn't really…agreed to, you know. Have a child with you?"

"Of course he agreed," said Gina, eyes on her cereal.

"So you're going to get married."

"I *said* we were."

"When?" said Heather, her Cheerios floating soggily in the bottom of her bowl.

"After he graduates," said Gina. "You know. In June. I'll be a June bride."

Heather did a muzzy calculation. It was the middle of March now. March, April, June.

Which meant Gina was due…July, August. In September. She rubbed her eyes. The timing would be tight between birth and death. First children were often overdue. Gina had been a week and a half late. By some miracle, could she, Heather, last until October? Already she felt exhausted.

The doorbell rang.

"I gotta go," said Gina, and shoved her chair back.

"No," said Heather. "Bring him in. I want to meet him. I want to talk to him."

"We'll be late for school."

"Just…" Heather made helpless motions with her hands. "Just bring him in."

Gina gave a big, dramatic shrug. "O*kay*," and went to answer the door. *Come on,* Heather heard her say. *My mom wants to talk to you.* There was an inaudible pause, and then Gina said, *Yeah. She knows.*

Danny was a skinny dude. Dude was the only word Heather could come up with for him as he came down the stairs and into the kitchen. He looked older than eighteen. He had a scruffy beard just covering his chin. It must've been a cold morning because his neck tats were covered by the collar of his leather jacket. Heather tried hard to see what it was in him that had attracted her daughter. She swallowed in a dry, Percocet mouth. Maybe it was his personality.

"Sit down," she said, gesturing to Jack's chair. "Would you like some coffee? Or some tea—I don't think we have any coffee. Have you had breakfast?"

He looked at the chair, but he didn't sit. "Uh," he said. "Thanks, but we're already late."

"Look," said Heather. "I know Gina's pregnant. You're going to sit, and we're going to talk about that. I don't care how late you are."

He blinked and sat. "Okay."

Gina sat next to him. Her face had changed to a flat, defensive mask.

"So," said Heather. "I barely know you and I'm going to be your mother-in-law. Tell me something about yourself."

"Well, uh," said Danny. "I'm, like, a senior. I have a job at Morgan's Welding. It pays twelve bucks an hour." This last part he said with obvious pride.

Heather nodded. "Will they give you full-time when you graduate?"

"Uh," said Danny. "Uh-huh." He glanced at Gina as though checking to see if that was the right answer.

"Have you figured out how much you'll need to save to take care of the baby?" said Heather. "And do they give you health insurance at Morgan's?"

"Uh," said Danny. "I don't really know about the health insurance? And, um, yeah, we're saving for the baby."

"Are you?" said Heather. "How much do you have so far? I mean, in the bank."

"In the bank?" echoed Danny. "Man, I have to pay for my car. If I don't have a car, I can't get to work."

Heather rubbed her eyes against the onslaught of the drugs. "What kind of car do you have?"

"It's a primo '97 TransAm," he said proudly. "Black satin finish, dual exhaust. Three-fifty engine. You know." He elbowed Gina, who allowed herself to smile. "Bitchin."

"How much do you pay every month?" said Heather.

"Two hundred bucks," said Danny. "Until December of next year. The guy who sold it to me was real reasonable. He didn't charge me no interest."

Heather looked at her dissolving cereal. "How much do you have left after you pay for the car?"

He let out a bark of a laugh. "Nothin, man."

"So how're you going to support Gina and a baby?"

"Huh?" said Danny. "We're gonna live at my mom's house. She's pumped about this. I got that covered."

"Does *she* have health insurance?"

"I guess," said Danny. "I mean we don't go to the doctor for, like, a little sniffle or anything."

"A *baby* isn't like a 'sniffle.'" said Heather. "It costs thousands of dollars to have a baby. In a *hospital*, with a *doctor*. And that's not counting prenatal care."

Danny looked at Gina. "My mom had me in a taxicab. She tell you that?"

Maybe he was good in bed, but Heather doubted it. "Are you listening to me?"

"Sure I am," said Danny, "but I think you're worrying too much." His tongue darted out to lick his lips as she scowled at him. "I mean I know you're like, dying and stuff. I mean. You know. You probably worry about everything right now."

And that was as close to sympathy as she was ever going to get from him. "You're going to marry my daughter," snapped Heather. "You're going to stay with her and your child and never leave. *And* you're going to ask your boss about health insurance. *Today.*"

"I don't go in today," said Danny.

"Then call him," said Heather. "And when you come by here tomorrow, I want an answer."

"Jesus, Mom, get off his back."

"Gina," said Heather, "I haven't even gotten started."

"Shit," said Danny. "I guess it's true what they say about

mother-in-laws." Outside, a car horn honked impatiently. He got up. "We gotta go."

Heather watched the two of them leave. When the door shut behind them, she put her face in her hands and sobbed.

LATER, after a long sleep, when she felt capable of cleaning up the kitchen, Heather opened the dishwasher to find it full of dirty dishes. That was defeating. She poured in powdered soap and washed the spaghetti sauce-caked dishes by hand.

She scrubbed half-heartedly. Shouldn't this be Jack's job? What about Gina? Shouldn't she be learning how to keep house? On the other hand, she would be living with Danny's mother. Would Danny's mother teach her how to cook something other than spaghetti and meatballs? Why hadn't Heather taught her daughter things, such as making a salad? Budgeting for a family? Doing the basics, like the laundry? She'd always thought she would have more time. And Gina was still enjoying her childhood. At least until now. Heather scrubbed at the stubborn red stains until her stitches hurt. She should make a plan, a list, maybe even a video of how to be a housewife. Because what else would Gina ever be? It would be a miracle if she finished high school with a baby. An even bigger miracle if she went to community college to become an X-ray technician. Gina closed her eyes and prayed to an unknown god that Danny would turn out to be a good and faithful husband. That having a child would give Gina the motivation to improve her life. That her own death would be painless, and free of doubts. This last part was a futile wish and she knew it, but she prayed for it anyway.

THAT AFTERNOON, Gina shook her awake. By the bedside clock, it was four.

"Mom? Mom. Are you up for some company? Someone's here to see you."

"Who?" she mumbled. Who on earth?

"It's Danny's mom. Her name's Mary. She came over to talk to you."

Heather pushed herself up in bed. Her hair felt like it was a shambles. She had fallen asleep in her bathrobe and a T-shirt. "She can't see me like this."

"You want to take a shower and put on some clothes?" Gina didn't seem impatient. She looked relieved. "She's here for dinner. She'll wait."

"Dinner?" echoed Heather. "I'm not in any shape to cook."

"We're cooking," said Gina. "Me and Mary. We went and got groceries. Everything's all set."

"Where's your father?"

Gina shrugged. "Still at work?"

"Oh." Heather edged carefully out of the bed and onto her feet. Her mind was one vast blur. She couldn't feel anything. "I'll take a shower," she said. "I'll be right there."

THE SHOWER felt good. Her hair *was* a shambles. She stood in front of the mirror, with the big pink bath towel wrapped around her diminished chest, feeling hollow-eyed, pale in the lips. Danny's mom, Mary. Was this what she would see? Ugh. Heather put on some lipstick, smacked it into place, and went to find some clothes.

MARY WAS A FAT, smiling little woman, with the same dark hair as her son. Danny was sitting at the kitchen table drinking a Coke, while Gina and Mary did things with the stove. The kitchen smelled like roasting chicken, which made Heather's dry mouth water. Something was boiling and something else was steaming. Could it be potatoes and broccoli?

"Hi," she said from the kitchen door.

"Mom!" said Gina, as though she was surprised to see her.

"Mrs. North," said Mary, and came over with a bit of a waddle. "I'm Mary Baker, Danny's mom."

"Please," said Heather, "call me Heather."

They shook hands awkwardly, and Mary, even more awkwardly, gave Heather a light hug. "Oh, honey," she said. "Sit down and I'll get you something to drink. You want water? Tea?" She nodded toward her son. "A Coke? We got a 12-pack. There's plenty of everything."

Heather sat gingerly. "I think a Coke would be great. Thanks."

Mary bustled around the kitchen, getting a glass, ice, a can of Coke. It was like she'd been here before and already knew where everything was. Heather's head buzzed with amazement.

"I'll have one, too," said Mary. "We can sit and chat for a while. The chicken's got another fifteen, twenty minutes. Gina's got everything else under control, don't you baby?"

Gina nodded brightly. Danny took a sip of Coke and eyed Heather over the rim of his glass. Heather wondered where the hell Jack was.

Mary sat down next to Heather and put the Coke in front of her. "Have some of this," she said. "It'll wake you up a little."

Heather drank slowly but deeply. The fizz drenched her mouth and nose. It cleared the thick space behind her forehead. It filled her mouth so she didn't have to speak just yet.

"So," said Mary, watching her drink. "I'm glad we could finally meet. Seeing as we'll be in-laws soon."

Heather swallowed. "Yeah," she said. "I'm glad you came. To be honest, I don't know Danny very well, and when Gina told me they were going to get married...and, um, have a baby. Well. I was pretty surprised." She looked at Danny as she said this, to see what his reaction would be. Danny's expression didn't change. He didn't even blink. It was like he hadn't even heard her.

"Well," said Mary, sounding apologetic. "I guess I've known about the baby for about a month now. And we know Gina real well. She spends a lot of time at the house. Doing homework and whatever."

And whatever. Heather took another drink.

"Gina didn't tell you about the baby," said Mary, "because you were so sick. She didn't want to add stress to your life."

Gina was at the stove, back turned, giving no sign that she'd heard. It was like being in a room full of deaf people, thought Heather. Maybe she could say anything she liked.

"I am really sick," she said. "Did Gina tell you what my doctor said?"

Mary nodded. Sadly? Sympathetically? There was something else there, though, that Heather couldn't quite identify.

"So," she said to Mary, "tell me about yourself and your family. Where do you live? What do you do?"

"Well," said Mary, still smiling, but shyly now, "it's just me and Danny, you know. Danny's dad ran off when he was only four, so it's just been him and me. I work at Westridge Elementary."

"You're a teacher?" said Heather, with an incredible burst of hope.

"I'm in the cafeteria," said Mary. "I'm one of the lunch ladies. Of course, we make breakfast, too, for the kids who come in extra early." She kept smiling, as though breakfast was a fond memory. "Danny and I live just down the street from the school."

Westridge wasn't exactly an up-and-coming neighborhood. It was maybe two square miles of post-war slab housing. The trees, planted sixty years ago when the houses were new, were huge and shady, but the houses were falling apart now and most of them were rentals. Heather had interviewed for a job as a first grade teacher at Westridge Elementary, years ago. They had rejected her, saying she didn't have enough experience with low-income students. She had thought at the time, *what bullshit.* Now she looked at Danny and wondered what kind of first-grader he'd been. What she would have done with him.

"You know," said Heather, "my husband is having an affair." She swallowed hard. Mary stopped smiling. "I don't know how long he'll be around for Gina. Or the baby. I mean he wants her to go to community college. But I don't know. I don't know." Heather blinked back tears and drank some more Coke, but the fizz had gone flat and the syrupy flavor just made her want to weep.

Mary patted her hand, then gripped it firmly. That made everything worse. Heather put her head on the table and began to cry.

Danny said, "Whoa."

Gina said, "Mom?"

"Get out of the kitchen, kids," said Mary, with authority. "Both of you."

Gina said, "But the chicken…"

"Out," said Mary, "now."

Danny scraped the chair back and the two of them left the room. In a minute, their feet were going up the stairs.

Heather cried harder. The deaf people were gone. It was safe to let go. She felt her hot tears actually pooling on the butcher-block table. She sat up and rubbed her face like a six-year-old, snot dribbling down to her upper lip. Was her lipstick smearing? Oh God.

"There, there," said Mary. "There, there."

"I'm so fucking scared for her," gasped Heather. "I'm so fucking scared." For herself. She knew this was the sort of thing she should be telling someone who would guide her gently through the Stages, not with this stranger, whose best attempt was going to be *there, there*. "I don't know what to do," she wept. "I mean, what's Gina going to do with a *baby*? She's barely sixteen."

"I was seventeen when I had Danny," said Mary softly. "Even though his dad left, we were okay. We managed. I stayed with my parents for a while, but I had jobs. I kept food on the table. What about Gina's grandparents? Wouldn't they help her out?"

"My parents died together in an accident, about ten years ago." Heather sniffed hard. Tears were rolling down her face on their own now. More sobbing wouldn't stop them. Neither would trying not to cry. They were just going to be there. Lots of tears. "My folks were going to set up a trust fund for Gina, but they never got around to it." She wiped her eyes with the heels of her hands. "Jack's parents were very strict with him when he was growing up. They never liked the way I was raising Gina. I mean, they'd take her, but they wouldn't want the, the baby."

"Not even a great-grandchild?" said Mary.

Heather pushed her hair back. "I should call and tell them what's going on. But what do I say? I'm dying and your granddaughter is pregnant at sixteen? Here, please take her?"

Mary squeezed Heather's hand. "They don't have to take her. My Danny's going to marry her. They might want to send some cash to help out, that's all."

"Oh my God," said Heather. "To help out with what? His car payments? Isn't that where all his money goes?" She grabbed Mary's plump shoulders. She wanted to shake this woman into awareness. "He doesn't have anything!"

Mary's face creased into a frown. "You think he's going to leave her. Just like his daddy did."

Heather pulled her hands back. "What if he does? What's she supposed to do then?"

Mary studied her, and for the first time, Heather wondered how old she was. If she was seventeen when she'd had Danny, and Danny was eighteen now...then Mary was an aged-looking thirty-five. Heather could picture her in the net cap and white apron that all lunch ladies wore. Mary's steel-gray eyes stared back at her, no doubt judging, no doubt reading her drug-addled thoughts.

"You know," Mary said, "when Danny was little, he was so smart, I thought he'd be able to do anything with his life.

He could've joined the army, got his college paid for. Been a pilot, anything. But then he got this welding job and he's happy. It pays for his car—and he loves that car almost as much as he loves Gina—it pays part of the rent. I had, you know, expectations for him. But he's got his own expectations, and I can't get in his way. You have expectations for Gina."

"I did," said Heather weakly. "I wanted her to go to college. She could be so much more than—than…"

"A teen mom?" said Mary quietly.

Heather let her breath out. She'd insulted this woman. This woman who was going to watch out for Gina. "She's still a *child*."

"She wants to give you a gift," said Mary. "And I'm telling you, you need to be grateful for that gift."

"Because that's all I'm going to be able to get from her," whispered Heather, "before I die."

"I wasn't going to say that," said Mary, "but it's one way of looking at it."

"What did your parents do when you told them you were pregnant?" said Heather. "Were they supportive?"

"They kicked me bang out of the house," said Mary. She put her hands in her lap. "So I married Nick."

Heather closed her eyes. Gina's options whirled behind her eyelids, making her dizzy and sick to her stomach. "Look," she said, and opened her eyes again. "Will you promise me something?"

"I will if I can."

"If—if Danny decides he's better off without her, will you be sure she's all right? As one mom to another. I don't want my little girl to be homeless or hungry." Now the tears were starting again.

"And I wouldn't want my grandchild to be homeless or hungry," said Mary. The frown was gone, the smile was gone. What was left was a concerned face, a youngish woman, someone who knew what it was to be abandoned. A face just like Gina was going to have one of these days, as she said these exact same words to her own daughter. Heather reeled at the vision of her child's future and shut her eyes against it. More tears leaked out.

"There, there," said Mary, still holding her hand. "There, there."

Footsteps sounded on the stairs. Heather wiped her eyes and smoothed her hair as the kids came back into the kitchen.

Gina peered at her. "Are you all right, Mom?"

It was an inane question. "Yes," sniffed Heather. "I'm fine." An equally inane answer.

"Come on, Danny," said Gina. "Help me with the chicken."

Danny didn't say anything, but glanced at Heather and his own mother, then followed Gina to the stove. Together they manhandled the chicken out of the oven. Gina dumped out the boiling potatoes. Danny forked broccoli out of the steaming pot. They didn't look natural together, Heather thought. Her daughter was well-groomed and pretty. Danny wasn't either one of those things. *At least,* she told herself, *he'll graduate from high school. At least he has a job.* She watched critically as he knifed the chicken apart and put it on a plate. Gina put the potatoes in one bowl and the broccoli in another. Together they brought the food to the table like an offering.

"Looks delicious," said Mary. "Honey," she said to Heather. "Do you think you can eat?"

Heather nodded, not trusting her voice. Danny put a plate in front of her, with the knife, fork, and spoon all on one side, and a folded paper towel on the other. He sat down in Jack's chair, Gina to his right, his mother to his left and Heather straight across. For the first time, Heather got a chance to look right into his eyes. They were brown and soft, like Jack's, and maybe that's what Gina had seen in him. They weren't a welder's eyes. They weren't a liar's eyes. They weren't the eyes of a man who would run off and leave his family, but Heather knew he would. The baby would have those eyes and would always remind Gina of him as he came and went and came and went.

Heather looked down at the empty white plate on the butcher-block table. Mary would be the constant in her daughter's life. It was Mary who would teach her how to cook and clean and watch over the baby. It would be Mary who would show her how to hold down two jobs at once and still have time for the kid. It was Mary who knew the things that Gina would need to learn, not her, not Heather and her expectations of college and some kind of success in life.

The realization made her slump into her chair with something like relief.

On one side, Mary took her hand. Suddenly, on the other, were Gina's warm fingers.

"Let's bow our heads now and say grace," said Mary, and without waiting, she went on to pray for all of them.

The Lapedo Child

MORTON SHAWN BROWN got off the train from Porter-ville. In Porterville he'd gotten off the train from Biloxi. In Biloxi he'd gotten off the train from Savannah, and before that, many trains earlier, he'd gotten on a train in Boston, to leave his family for the year. They were too poor during this depression to give him anything for his sixteenth birthday except fare to the southern end of Mississippi, where his cousins, almost as poor, awaited him.

These cousins, from his mother's side, were called Smith. Browns were common enough in Boston, high and low, but when his cousins picked him up from this final station in a mule cart, he could see that these Smiths fit right in among whatever else had sunk to the bottom. They put him and his two suitcases in the back and said nothing to him except that he should expect to earn his keep.

They told him he'd be chopping wood, mucking the sta-ble, lending a hand with the farm, and so on, which made him wonder, half aloud, how they'd gotten along without him. If his cousins Marjorie and James heard him, they ignored him and didn't say another thing until they got to their sagging two-story farmhouse. James stopped the mule, and Morton unloaded his belongings. Marjorie showed him to his room upstairs and left him there to change into work clothes, which he didn't have, so she gave him some of James's.

James showed him how to muck a stall, how to clean up after the two starving dairy cows, and then how to split kindling for the woodstove. After supper, which was cold and meager, he lay on the hard cot they had given him, watching the moon rise into the spring Mississippi sky, and decided that he could not stay.

The following day he chopped wood until his hands blistered inside the gloves James had given him. That's how soft his hands were. The sun was barely hitting the tops of the trees. His breakfast of bread and shortening lay in his stomach. He thought of how he'd played cards at lunch in school and won sometimes, and wondered if he could run away to become a gambler. The problem with running was that when he looked at the area around the house he saw piney woods on one side, which James had intimated they would be cutting into fairly soon. He saw the yet-to-be-planted corn and cotton fields behind him. On the other side was a sloping hill that rolled down to the ruins of a large plantation house. In front of the house was the road. That was all. If he wanted to go, he would have to leave his luggage, his clothes, everything, and walk off as a thief, with a pair of James's coveralls and gloves.

HE STAYED for two weeks. His hands got a little harder but his body hurt like hell every night and every day. When he and James sawed down the first of the tall pine trees, the tree nearly fell on top of him and James laughed when Morton shrieked, high-pitched like a girl. It occurred to Morton as he scampered backward from the still-shuddering trunk that he could laugh too and things might be easier for him, but the thought passed. He was too young to be so mature, and nothing in the hardness of the work or the meanness of the life there would change that.

His chance to leave came one morning as he chopped kindling. He heard cart wheels and hoofbeats and when he looked up, a mule was wandering past the house with an empty cart behind it. Morton ran up to the mule and stopped it. In the cart were a small black bag and two neatly rolled blankets. Morton put down the ax, just left it on the ground. He took off the gloves and threw them beside it. He got up into the cart and took the reins. He slapped the mule, which broke into a trot, and in moments he was running away, the sagging house behind him, the dusty dirt road stretching ahead.

After a long while, the mule came to a river and stopped. Morton wasn't sure how deep the river was, but there were other wagon tracks in the mud on the other side, as though others had waded on through. Other roads had intersected with this one and it had become wider, more traveled looking, which made Morton a little nervous. The mule was brownish black, sleek, with a white splash on its face. Anyone who saw it would know it in particular. While it was drinking from the river, he opened the black bag in the cart and saw medicine bottles, silver tweezers, tiny scissors, a roll of very fine gauze. He guessed this was a doctor's cart, the doctor's mule, and that anyone would know that he was stealing it.

He had done his share of thieving in Boston, but nothing like this. He had stolen candy as a child, stolen a shirt from a store once when he was fourteen, had once made false change off a very stupid girl behind a counter and ended up with a dime more than he had going in. He had friends in school who considered themselves skilled, if not professional, thieves. They'd invited him to help them with different scams, including one involving breaking into one of their teachers' houses. He'd drawn the line there for himself. His father would have beaten him if he'd stepped over that line, and his father was not a man prone to beating.

Morton had only the sense of honor of a sixteen-year-old, which was more a dread of getting caught. If he went back, James would beat him. James did not seem like a man who would hesitate to raise a hand in anger, though Morton had never seen him do anything violent. Morton raised the reins and slapped the vagrant mule into the water and across to the other side.

As the afternoon came on, the road, canopied with wide oak branches, was cool in the heat of midday. Occasionally the branches would part and sunlight would pool on the dirt, forming bright, disorienting spots in the distance. The bright spots became mirages and shimmered like water in the middle of the road. It was from one of these watery bright spots that a man emerged, walking quickly toward Morton and the mule cart. When the man was close enough, Morton saw that he was a Negro wearing a waistcoat. The man waved energetically and stopped where he was, waiting.

The mule snorted as though in recognition.

Now, thought Morton despondently, now comes my just reward.

The Negro man put a hand into his pocket and produced an apple, and the mule picked up its pace. Since there was no use in pretending, Morton let the reins go until the man caught the bridle and stopped the mule.

"You've found him," said the Negro. "Thank God. Elijah," he said to the mule, "how rude to trouble this young man!"

Morton had never spoken to a Negro, only seen them and heard what his Boston friends, and his Mississippi cousins, said about them. It only occurred to him slowly that this well-dressed Negro man with new but dusty shoes was the doctor. It occurred to him with equal slowness that the man had come from the wrong direction. Wouldn't he have been chasing the mule from behind? It came to him that the well-dressed Negro might be as much a thief as he was.

"If this is your mule," said Morton, "how did you pass him? How're you coming from in front rather than behind?"

"He's heading home, of course," said the man. "There're plenty of shortcuts hereabouts, young sir." He frowned at Morton. "You're new here. You're the young man from the Smith place."

"How do you know that?"

"Your accent, sir," said the Negro and made a slight bow. "I am Doctor Clarence Miller, doctor to the coloreds in these parts." He made to climb up into the seat of the wagon, but Morton didn't move.

"How do I know this is your wagon? This mule was just wandering."

A shadow of real impatience passed over the Negro's face. "My medical bag, young man, and two blankets in the back. Did you find those?"

Morton hesitated but nodded.

"Now let me up, young man," said the doctor. "You're welcome to come along, but I have a baby to deliver yet today."

He climbed up into the wagon, took the reins, and slapped the mule. The driver's bench was narrow and the doctor was not a thin man. The mule broke into a trot and the wagon lurched forward. Morton felt he might pitch off at any moment and gripped the edge of the bench.

"Where, if I may ask," said the doctor after a few minutes, "were you heading with Elijah and my cart?"

"I don't know," said Morton.

"Just leaving?" said the doctor. "Just leaving your cousins?"

"Just leaving," said Morton.

"They work you hard," said the doctor, not unsympathetically. "You didn't like it."

"I didn't like it," said Morton. "They must have been able to get along without me before. They'll get along without me now."

"It isn't fair," agreed the doctor, "to get you all the way down here and then make you work for nothing more than a room with a hard bed."

"It isn't fair," said Morton, surprised. "How do you know all this?"

"It's a common practice," said the doctor. "People send for family in these hard times and think they're doing a favor by putting them to hard labor. I imagine you could have made your way staying at home up north. You look like an intelligent young man. Certainly they didn't have to send you way down here."

"We didn't have enough money to feed everyone," said Morton. "At least on a farm the food grows right there. But all my cousins were giving me was bread for breakfast, old potatoes for lunch, and bread and some parts of a pig for supper."

"And your cousins," said the doctor. "They ate better than you."

"They had better parts of the pig. I know that."

"In the spring," said the doctor, "we call it the starving time. Nothing's grown enough yet to harvest. Everyone's eating the last of what's been buried in baskets under the floor of the barn or hung in the smokehouse." He slowed the mule, and for a moment Morton thought the man would turn around and take him back to his cousins.

"I'm not going back there," he said fiercely, but the doctor gave him a mild look and turned the mule off the road onto a barely visible track that led into the woods. After a moment a sagging gray shack came into view. A barking dog ran out. Children dark as the mule looked up as the doctor approached, and one of the oldest ran to catch the reins. Morton counted a dozen children, each a year older and half a head taller than the last, the youngest barely walking. Smoke curled up from a rickety chimney. The yard was bare dirt and scattering chickens. Somewhere a donkey brayed. From behind the house two barefoot young women emerged, their clothes thin, patched, shiny with wear.

The doctor swung down from the wagon, leaving Morton

strangely visible yet invisible in the middle of things, a glaringly white distraction from the birth of another baby but not important enough to eclipse it. He gathered from the conversation below him that the baby had already been born but the mother was having some trouble. He didn't understand all the words, which were like another language compared to the accents of his cousins.

The doctor disappeared behind the house with the two young women, leaving the rest of the children and the boy holding the reins to stare at the white man sticking up from the wagon and the yard like a thumb, the likes of which they'd never seen before in their young lives. No one even offered him water.

LATER, toward dusk, back in the wagon and on the main road, the doctor offered to drop Morton off in the town of Lapedo, which was only a few miles off and not far out of his way. Morton had no money, nothing but the stolen clothes on his back, and of course knew no one in the town of Lapedo. He said all this to the doctor.

"I'll introduce you to the butcher," he said. "He's a white man, but a friend of mine. I've stitched him up plenty of times. I know he's talked of needing an apprentice. If farm work's not for you, you could try a trade." He cocked his head at Morton. "A butcher always eats."

"What about you?" said Morton. "Do you always eat?"

Doctor Miller shrugged. He didn't have even the shadow of starvation about him. "People pay me in hens and roosters, sometimes in ham. Sometimes in boots. It just depends, but generally, yes sir, I eat."

"Do you need an apprentice?" Morton asked boldly.

Miller let out a laugh of surprise. "I have a son, young sir, but the butcher, Samuels, has daughters. He needs a boy. You'd do worse than a trade like that."

Morton didn't know how he felt about blood and gore. A friend in Boston had rabbits, which he killed with a stick. No doubt the butcher dealt with larger animals. He wondered if he could get used to it, if it would be harder than chopping down a forest for firewood.

"All right," he said, as though Miller had offered him a choice between one thing and another.

Samuels, the butcher, lived in a small brick house in the town of Lapedo. His shop, Samuels Meats, was next door. The barn for the doomed animals was behind that. In the evening, cattle lowed.

The two of them went around to the back of Samuels's house, where a Negro maid met them at the door. She greeted Miller warmly. She seemed on the verge of inviting them in when she saw Morton's dirty coverall and offered the two of them sandwiches on the back porch instead.

Samuels came back from the front of the house. He was a short white man, broad across the shoulders, thick in the waist. He was missing two fingers on his left hand. His sleeves were rolled up and Morton could see scars on his forearms, which looked like he'd been attacked with knives.

Miller introduced Morton. Morton shook the butcher's hand, something he realized he had yet to do with Miller. The doctor brought up the possibility of apprenticeship. Samuels, who still had Morton's hand in his grip, squeezed hard, like a test of strength. Hardened by chopping wood and mucking stalls, Morton squeezed back. The butcher released him. He asked a few questions about Morton's family, discovered he was a cousin of the Smiths, and nodded as though he completely understood why Morton was standing on the steps of his back door.

"It won't be easy work," he said. "There's a lot of blood." To Miller he said, "I'll give him two weeks."

Miller raised a hand in farewell. "I'll tell your family where you are," he said.

"Thank you," said Morton and reached for his hand to shake it, but the doctor was already turning away.

Because he was dirty, but mostly because of the daughters, Morton slept in the barn in the loft above the cows and pigs.

THE NEXT DAY Samuels showed him how to sharpen a knife, and started him on stripping the hide off the corpse of a cow that had probably died of hunger, its ribs were so profound. It struck Morton as he cut the skin away with as little damage as he could that it was a little like peeling an orange. He had heard that if you were careful you could pull the skin from an orange in one piece, lay it flat on the table, and see how Earth would look if it were flattened. The cow was spotted black and white, and he wondered what shapes the blacks and whites would make if they could be put together as contiguous but separate parts. This was what he thought about as he peeled the skin away.

He was good enough at skinning that it became his job. One of the butcher's three daughters showed up to help with scalding the hair off the hogs after they had been slaughtered. She was not a beautiful girl, and except for the big jobs that required a crew of hands she stayed away from her father's business and went to school in town. Her looks aside, she dressed nicely and was polite to Morton.

He ate well and was paid enough for his work that he could buy himself some new clothes. On his day off, he walked through the town of Lapedo. The town wasn't big but it had a general store, a druggist, a bar, a laundry, and train tracks that ran right through the middle. The train didn't stop unless someone stood on one side of the tracks and waved it down. Morton watched this from the bar on his day off and thought of Boston, but there was no way he could go back.

The bartender, who ignored the fact that Morton was underage, asked if he wanted another beer. The beer was cheap and watery. Morton already knew what beer was supposed to taste like, which made him homesick for his friends and the bottle parties under the bridge by the river. He put down a nickel and the bartender brought him his second beer of the afternoon. It was Sunday and half the male population of the town was here drinking away the effects of morning church. The other half were sitting down to Sunday supper with their families, which was what Samuels the butcher was doing right now. Morton hadn't been invited to sit down with the family, which was fine with him. It was his second Sunday in Lapedo, and he could see that the bar might easily become his home in his off-hours. He was sitting at the bar itself, which was a liquor-stained plank lined with a variety of stools. The rest of the bar was essentially a narrow hallway filled with chairs and tables. In Boston there would have been a jukebox. Here there was a radio tuned, incongruously, to gospel music. In

Boston, his friends would have found their way in and commandeered a table. Here, dogs lay on the floor while their masters slumped over their cups in their Sunday best or shouted at each other about the state of the weather, the government, or the coloreds.

The local boys, though, did have their own table. They had eyed him last weekend. They were a tough-looking bunch, chewing tobacco, big handed and rednecked. Morton already knew his name was a handicap. He'd managed to make it an asset in Boston, but it had taken a lot of proving of himself from the time he was small. Here he was a foreigner with a funny name. Acceptance didn't look like a readily available thing. He turned back to his watery beer with its tender froth and took a long swig.

NOT LONG AFTERWARD he cut his hand on the razor-sharp knife while he was peeling the hides from cows, and a doctor was called. Because he was the cheapest of the doctors, Miller, the colored man, came in. Miller clucked over the slice, which ran across Morton's right palm. It couldn't be stitched but had to be wrapped with gauze and soaked with ointment, and using it was out of the question for at least a week. Samuels swore at Morton, which Morton took as a positive sign that he was needed, but he cringed under the ferocity of it. Samuels paid Miller with a couple of steaks and stormed out of the cold cutting shed. Morton clumsily wrapped the meat with white paper and string while Miller watched.

"Being a butcher," said Miller, "is about being cut."

"I doubt if he'll feed me while I'm cut," said Morton.

"Where do you sleep?" said Miller.

"In the barn."

"Well," said Miller. "He won't kick you out of there, but he won't want you around much, either. Why don't you come with me on my rounds today? I could use the conversation."

Morton had heard everything anyone in the bar and the butcher shop had said about the coloreds in Lapedo County, and Miller's name came up often enough.

"What would people say?" said Morton without much feeling.

"I think you know what they'll say," said Miller.

MORTON, once again in the mule cart, away from the smell of freshly killed creatures, felt a wash of relief in the cool June afternoon. He'd changed out of his bloody work coverall into a shirt and pants he'd bought in town, but his shoes were still caked with the offal of the butcher's killing floor. The mule seemed to sense this, and Miller made Morton sit in the back of the cart.

"Tell me about your family," said Miller. "You must be the youngest, to get sent down here, down the river, so to speak."

Morton didn't understand the reference but he nodded. "I have three older brothers and two sisters. My sisters are still home, but everyone else is grown and gone."

"And no one could take you on up north?" said Miller. "There was no work at all?"

"I couldn't work for my brothers," said Morton. "One runs a sawmill, one makes bricks, one's a banker. After the crash, none of them had anything. My mother takes in sewing and washing to make money."

"And what does your pap do?"

"He used to paint houses, but even that's hard work to get anymore."

"And what did you do before you became a butcher's assistant?"

Morton shrugged. "I painted houses. I would've done what my father did. I would've done anything if there'd been anything to do."

"But not farming."

"That wasn't farming," said Morton. "That was just, well, labor." He didn't want to say *slavery*. Though they hadn't passed anyone on the road all afternoon, he was aware that sitting in the back like this, it might appear that Miller was driving him, like a man of some leisure, around the county for whatever reason. The thought didn't exactly make him uncomfortable—it was anything but leisurely in the back of the wooden cart—but he was surprised to find himself concerned about appearances.

Miller turned the mule off the main road onto one that might have been a riverbed at one time and probably returned to that state when it rained hard. The red mud was pocked with big stones. Morton got out when Miller stopped the cart to inspect one of the wheels, and when they started up again, he told Miller he preferred to walk. The washed-out road was wide enough for him to walk abreast of the wagon, and the mule was going slow, so it was easy to talk.

"What else did you leave behind in Boston?" said Miller, drawing the word out, *Bah*-ston, like Morton did. "Girls? Friends?"

"My friends from school," said Morton. "I guess there was a girl or two." He paused but Miller didn't say anything and looked like he was waiting for the rest of some story. Conversation, Morton finally realized, was entertainment to fill these long stretches of travel with the mule, and was not necessarily a two-way conversation.

"Well," he said, "there was a girl name of Anna. Really pretty girl, a grade ahead of me, so I didn't have any chance with her, but I did like looking at her."

"She ever look your way?"

"Not ever," said Morton, "but she was nice—blonde—" he made a few shy, vague gestures around his chest and hips, and Miller let out a laugh. "She had friends who tried to look as good as she did, but they never matched up to her. I had a friend who tried to take her to the carnival once. He went over to her house to invite her and all he got was her father standing in the door. He got smart with her dad and her dad punched him right in the nose."

Miller laughed again. "What did you do with your friends for entertainment, since you had such bad luck with the girls?"

"Not much," said Morton. "To tell you the truth there wasn't much we could do. My friends needed work. Our families weren't rich. Sometimes we stole." He paused, ashamed he'd admitted this. "But not for fun," which was a lie. He stopped, wondering if Miller could sense lies, the way his own father could so easily, or if Miller cared. Maybe it was just the story he wanted, embellished with anything.

"You stole," said Miller, without outrage. "I can't condone that sort of thing, of course, and can only warn you that habits like this developed in your youth, young sir, will not serve you well when you become a man."

"I only stole when I was with them," said Morton. "I haven't stolen anything here." But even that wasn't true. He had been prepared to make off with this very mule and cart, and if he hadn't run into Miller, he would likely be in some other state by now, on foot, having sold it for whatever he could get.

If Miller was thinking along these lines, he glossed over it. "The company you keep is important. Surely your father didn't approve of these friends."

"I was the youngest," said Morton honestly. "They didn't care who I was with as long as I stayed out of trouble. My mother always said that she was done with having children before I was born."

"So they let you run wild?" said Miller.

"Well, not exactly wild," said Morton. "I mean, I went to school. Most of the time. I didn't get into trouble, not very often. I didn't get caught very often, anyway." He eyed Miller to see if there was disapproval in his face, but Miller only grinned white teeth.

"How old is your son," said Morton, "the one who's going to follow in your footsteps?"

"He's eleven now." He said *now* as though he had almost forgotten how old his son was. "I have daughters too, twins. They're seven."

"Why doesn't your son come with you?"

"He's a little young for things I see and hear, young sir. I'm sure you've heard the things I refer to, and at Samuels's I know you see the same kinds of things I see myself. My son is a little too young yet for this world."

Morton didn't say anything. It seemed to him that the earlier a son was exposed to the death and hatred of the world, the sooner he would harden to it. He felt it had been that way with him. He had known from an early age that his mother considered him an extra burden and that his father had enough sons already to carry on the family business, if they chose, or to go into a trade that would support their parents in their old age. He had known for a long time that he wasn't actually wanted, and it had been a long time since he had wept about it.

"Where are you going today?" said Morton, to turn the subject away from himself.

"To see the widows," said Miller.

"How many widows are there around here?"

"You'd be surprised," said Miller. "This county breeds them. Their men are killed by falling trees, trampled by their own oxen, killed by white men. This is the week I see them all." He turned the mule to a fork angling right, and after a while the road became a series of deeper and deeper ruts. Trees hung closer to the wagon, and Miller got down from the bench and led the mule under the low-hanging branches.

"Which widow lives out here?" said Morton, because they were at least two hours from town now. The road was two grassy furrows in the ground, and the only sounds were birds singing madly in the branches of the oaks and maples.

"Widow Kale," said Miller. "Her husband used to work for the railroad."

"What happened to him?"

"No one's sure," said Miller. "He was found on the tracks between here and Jefferson, just dead, no signs of injury. It was like he'd died and fallen from the back of the caboose and no one noticed. He was a man who'd never had a sick day in his life. His wife, on the other hand, was always sickly. When they married, people worried about her chances in childbirth."

"Did they have children?"

"No, but she had her share of miscarriages. Now," said Miller, pulling the mule to a stop and looking Morton in the eye. "Young sir, I know I can rely on your discretion. Just because you and I are having this conversation doesn't mean that you need to share what you've heard from me with anyone else."

Morton thought of the conversations he'd heard in the bar. The only people who might care about what Doctor Miller was telling him were the butcher's daughters, and even they had no interest in a poor colored widow who lived in the middle of what was becoming a deep, humid forest.

"I promise," he said. "I won't say anything to anyone."

Miller gave a little snort. "Ridiculous of me. Which of the white folks would have any concern?" He tugged the mule's bridle. "Come, Elijah. It's not far now."

The widow's house was a pieced-together shack surrounded by a garden and not much bigger than the chicken coop built up next to it. The Widow Kale sat in an old kitchen chair on what might have been a front porch at one time but was now just a stretch of boards half-buried in the hard red clay.

Chickens scattered for Morton, Miller, and the mule. The Widow Kale stood. She was small, thin, and bent, but she didn't look as weak or sick as Morton had expected. Miller waved broadly and called to her in a very loud voice, and Morton realized she was probably mostly deaf.

Miller introduced Morton. Morton, not sure what else to do, gave her a respectful little bow. His own family was poor. He'd seen astonishing poverty around the town of Lapedo, but nothing he'd seen compared to the Widow Kale. The fabric of her dress had been patched and repatched. She was barefoot, and to his eyes it was unlikely that she'd ever worn a shoe. The house looked like it was held together with nails and old newspaper. Even the hens were thin, but their coop looked solid enough. To keep out foxes, of course. Any loss, even one chicken, would probably be a catastrophe. Morton looked back at the Widow Kale and caught her black, shiny eyes for a moment before she looked quickly away, like a furtive animal. Even old and weathered as she was, she reminded him of some woodland creature, hardly ever seen. Not exotic but familiar enough, like a mouse that only came out when nothing else was stirring, not even the singing birds.

She was offering to get cold water for them and Miller was jovially agreeing, but instead of going inside, she went to the far corner of the house and leaned on an iron pump until water came gushing out into a metal cup. She handed this to Morton first. The water was sweet and cold, probably the best of anything she could offer. He drank and gave the cup to Miller, who went over to the pump and filled the disintegrating trough underneath for the mule.

She didn't invite them inside and no one asked. She gave up her chair, which both Morton and Miller refused to take. Miller ended up sitting on a crate and Morton sat on the bench in the mule cart, not close enough to really be part of the conversation, which he could hardly understand once

Miller began speaking like a local. He watched the widow talk instead. Her mouth barely opened when she spoke, and Morton felt she was hiding her teeth from the doctor. He understood when Miller asked about her health, about her garden, about the health of the chickens. He gave her news of the Widow Owen, whom he'd seen before he'd come to bandage Morton's hand that afternoon. The conversation seemed mostly to flow out of Miller, and Morton had to admire how he made the old woman duck her head girlishly, with compliments about the state of the chickens and the garden, which was full of collards, onions, potatoes, and tomatoes just coming onto the vines. He understood when she said she was planning to can over the next week or two and invited the doctor to come back for a jar of mulberry and cherry preserves, which she would have ready for his next visit.

"That reminds me," said Miller, and motioned to Morton. "The steaks, young sir. They certainly won't travel any farther today in this heat."

Morton took the steaks out of the cart, still cool, seeping slightly through the butcher paper. He felt intensely awkward as he came toward the old woman, who bit her lips and looked away as he came closer with the meat. Miller scooped up the packages and handed them to her. It was at least six pounds of beef and she almost buckled under the weight when she took it from Miller.

"Compliments of Mister Samuels, the butcher," said Miller.

"Do thank him for me," said the Widow Kale, and without another word she turned and pushed open the door of her house and disappeared into the darkness inside. The door swung shut. Morton didn't even catch a glimpse of the interior.

Miller brushed off his hands and turned to Morton, smiling as though he didn't expect her to come back out. "Now," he said. "It's getting late, don't you think? We'll leave the other widows for tomorrow."

IT WAS EARLY in the evening when Miller dropped him off, a mile or so from town. It was an easy walk from the crossroads. Miller trotted the mule off in the opposite direction, not actually promising to see Morton the next day, but leaving the question open to interpretation.

Morton ate at the bar, drank a beer, and made his way back to Samuels's barn. It was well after dark, but Samuels must have seen him go in and came after him.

"Where've you been all day?" the butcher asked, as if he hadn't seen Morton get into Miller's cart that very morning.

"With the doctor," said Morton.

"You're not to go with him again," said Samuels. "I'll find you something to do, even with that cut."

Morton wanted to say he was grown enough to come and go as he pleased, but he didn't. He figured someone had said something to the butcher about the company his help kept. This was simply to control gossip. Mrs. Samuels probably had something to do with this, Morton thought. Having Morton in such close proximity to Miller might in turn have some effect on the desirability of the Samuels daughters. It was too complex for him to give much attention to. All he said was, "Yes sir," the way he would have spoken to his own father.

THE NEXT DAY he was assigned to scald the slaughtered hogs, which meant working with the oldest Samuels daughter, whose name was Emma. The work was heavy but not hard and didn't require more than one hand on his part. The hogs, freshly killed and gutted, were lowered from a block and tackle into a vat of boiling water to scald their hides and make it easier to remove the bristles. The bristles would be made into toothbrushes. Morton had a hog-bristle toothbrush, which he now wondered if he would ever use again. Still, he thought about the Widow Kale as Emma gave him a toothy but friendly smile; thought about how the old woman had hidden her teeth from the doctor even as he'd done his best to make her laugh. It was probably best to keep the toothbrush, he thought, and smiled back.

Emma was a stocky girl with her father's powerful build. Raising hogs on the block and tackle overhead and lowering them down seemed not much of a challenge for her. She could probably have done the work herself alone, but Morton tried manfully to help.

"I've cut myself like that," said Emma, nodding at his bandaged hand as they swung the next hog over the hot vat. They were working in a corner of the killing floor. The place smelled, as was normal, of blood and fear, but it was quiet except for the crackle of the fire under the vat and the sound of the cattle in the barnyard.

"Were you skinning?" Morton asked, to be polite. He was sure she had not been skinning, no matter how she was built. The job required a tallness she didn't have. Even her father had been standing on a stepladder when he had taught Morton the job.

"I was cutting apples for pie," said Emma. "I was doing it like this." She mimed holding an apple in her left palm and the knife in her right. "There's some things you just never do twice in your life."

It almost sounded like an invitation, so he thought for a moment about what he might be able to say. "What else?"

"Oh," she said, "I don't know. I used to think I'd stay here all my life. Now I wouldn't think twice about that. Now pull."

They hoisted the finished hog, dripping and smelling half-cooked, from the vat. The two of them rolled it along the pulley tracks to the other side of the floor, where her father would come shortly to put the carcasses in the meat locker. Emma disengaged the finished hog with an expert pull on the rope, and rolled the pulley along its tracks to fetch the next of the three they were supposed to do.

"Where do you think you'd go?" said Morton.

"I suppose anywhere my husband wanted to go," she said, "but I'd prefer somewhere with some snow. I've never seen snow. Have you?"

"In Boston?" said Morton. "We get a lot." He held a hand up to his chest to show how high it got. Her eyes widened.

"I've seen it in books," she said. "I've read about it. Is it very cold?"

"It depends," said Morton, and he thought about how odd it was to be talking about snow in a place as hot and foul as this. "Sometimes a Nor'easter comes in and dumps six feet, ten feet, and the weather's as cold as hell." He abruptly wondered if he should have said *hell* and looked around for Samuels, but Emma laughed.

"Hell is hot," she said. "*This*—" she gestured at the dead animals, the floor where the blood had been soaked up in sawdust—"*this* is hell."

"It gets real cold," said Morton, "whatever you want to say about it. And then we get wet snow, where it doesn't get quite cold enough. It gets to be slushy and turns black in the streets after a couple of days."

"I'd like to see snow," said Emma dreamily. She hooked the next hog and the two of them drew it over the vat. It took a moment of concentration to stop its swinging and make it come down straight so as not to make a splash in the boiling water. "I'd like to see snow no matter what color it was. You ever get blue snow?"

"No," said Morton. "Never heard of it, either."

"Green snow?"

Now she was just teasing him. "Nope," he said.

DOCTOR MILLER didn't come by that day or the next, and Morton spent the time trying to make himself useful around the Samuelses' house. Mrs. Samuels was a severe woman with gray hair she wore braided into a tight knot on the back of her head. Her clothes were so dark and old-fashioned, she almost looked like she was in perpetual mourning. The other two daughters, Molly and Bernice, who were only eight and nine, had the smaller jobs like sweeping and cleaning, and didn't work like their sister Emma in any aspect of their father's business. Mrs. Samuels finally gave Morton a stack of potatoes to peel, which he could do without reopening his wounded palm. In another few days he would be able to go back to work in the slaughterhouse, and as he sat peeling potatoes, he found that he didn't really relish the idea. He wondered where Miller was, if his tour of the widows of Lapedo County was done for the month, and what kind of catastrophe could have kept him from the pleasure of conversation with someone with so little to say as Morton. He had tried to make conversation with Mrs. Samuels, but she had even less to say than he could think of. She had no interest in snow, like her daughter, or the distant exoticism of Boston, like Miller.

July was nearly over and the heat of August had already settled over the house, the barn, and the deaths on the killing floor. There were times when Morton thought the animals might be grateful to be released, through a swift hammer blow to the skull, from the overpowering blister of the day. There were days when he would have welcomed it.

He didn't see Miller again until the end of August, when the weather broke with a series of heavy storms. His hand had healed well enough, and he had graduated from skinning to actual butchering. One day in the late summer, Miller arrived in the wind and drenching rain, practically clutching the seat of the cart to keep from getting blown off. He had driven around the back of Samuels's storefront to take shelter in the sheds where the cattle were.

Morton saw him and made his way through the downpour.

"There you are, young sir," said Miller, as though the weather were perfectly fine. "Please meet my son, Henry." He pulled open his slicker and Morton saw the boy crouched underneath, pushed up against his father, small and wide-eyed but mostly dry.

"Hello," said Morton.

The boy looked up at his father, who nodded. He turned to Morton and said, "Hello, mister" in such a flat and labored manner that Morton saw immediately why Miller didn't bring him along on his rounds. The boy was slow in the mind. He would never be able to replace his father, which meant that Miller would have to train someone else to take his place, if that was even possible in a place as poor and uneducated as this.

EVEN IN THE DAYS afterward, the idea that Miller had no kind of heir stuck with Morton. It wasn't as though he considered himself qualified or even a possible candidate to be the doctor to the coloreds of Lapedo County. It was that Miller's son was a disappointment, like himself.

THERE WAS A POINT, near Thanksgiving, when Morton thought he should go back to see his cousins. It had been six months since he'd arrived in Mississippi, and though he'd written to his parents he hadn't been in contact with Marjorie and James since he'd run off in Miller's mule cart. It was on the day that he was thinking about them, in mid-November, when they showed up at the butcher's with a cow that Morton didn't remember ever seeing on their small farm. They had brought it to be butchered and when they saw him with a pitchfork in the barn, they both looked surprised.

"Well," said James, "we thought you were in another state or dead by now."

Morton told them no, he'd just found a job that he was better suited for.

"What we heard," said Marjorie, "was that you was traveling with that colored doctor, Miller, but we didn't see how that was possible."

Morton just shrugged. It didn't matter to him what people thought about Miller any more, he suspected, than it mattered to Miller. "Not traveling," he said anyway. "Just helping him out some."

Samuels appeared, frowned at the Smiths, glanced at Morton, and seemed to put the three of them together. He came over and sized up the cow as well.

"What'll you charge," said James, "for the butchering?"

Samuels told him and James recoiled dramatically at the price, even though Morton knew it was reasonable for the size of the cow and the way it would have to be cut. It was a scrawny thing. Its bones would be the most nutritious part, and those would end up as soup.

Samuels and James bickered about the price and Marjorie came over close to Morton. She looked thinner to him. She said, "You look like you've been eatin'."

He wanted to tell her that part of what had made him run away was the parts of the pig she'd given him. "They feed me," he said.

"You sleep in the house," said Marjorie, "or do they put you in the barn with the dogs?"

He shrugged. He liked the dogs and didn't mind sleeping in clean straw. It was the feeling of doom in the barn that bothered him as he slept in the loft, but he didn't say anything about that.

"We got a letter from your folks," she said. "You know, they sent us money to take you in. After we told 'em you ran off, they wanted it back." She pushed a finger into his chest as though it was something she'd been wanting to do for some time. "*You* owe us now."

"For what?" he said, nonplussed. He didn't know there had been money involved.

"For the month you were with us." And she told him how much she expected. It was more than he had earned so far with the butcher.

Samuels and James finished haggling over the cost of killing the cow and dressing it out. It occurred to Morton that she was lying to him about the money and that his parents, strapped as they were, had never sent a dime, that this was just extortion from people who didn't even have the money to buy a decent cow. He found himself wanting to talk it over with Miller, but first he would write to his parents.

HE SPENT THE EVENING composing on a piece of butcher paper, with a pencil stub from the storefront where Samuels sold sausages, steaks, and sweetbreads. He realized he missed home more than he had thought. Instead of writing about the money, he found himself writing down and then erasing lines about the weather and the lack of friends here in the South, and how he missed the food of home. When he had filled up the paper, even scribbling around the edges, he folded it and put it under his rough, straw-filled pillow. He hadn't slept in a bed in six months, he realized, hadn't bathed regularly at all in that time, hadn't sat down to a table with his family. In spite of everything, he had become a fairly decent butcher's assistant. It was better, he knew, than the back-breaking labor he'd run away from, but when he thought of his brothers and his father, no matter how poor, he wondered if it wasn't time to go back. After all, he had a skill, if not a perfectly honed one. He rolled over in his bed of straw. Below, Marjorie and James's doomed cow lowed along with the rest. He thought of running away, at least long enough to find Miller, show him the letter, and ask his opinion about the money Marjorie said he owed. He wasn't sure where Miller lived, but he had a general idea. He'd heard people talk in the bar and knew the doctor had a brick house in the southwest corner of Lapedo County. The town of Lapedo itself was in the south-central part of the county, and it might be a two- or three-hour walk, if he could find the right roads. But by now he had a sense of the area, and a pretty good idea of where Miller lived in relation to the town.

He thought about Miller's son and young daughters and wondered how a man could expect to grow into old age without an heir of some kind. If it was him, he thought, he would try to have another son, not a superfluous child like himself, but one that could take over the family business—the childbirths, the medicine, the widows, the husbands found dead on the railroad tracks. It seemed deeply important for him to tell the doctor this, and he climbed down from the loft in the dark. He could be back before daylight.

THE MOON was mostly full and the sky was as clear as only a southern autumn night could be. In Boston there would have been frost and a bite to the air. Here it was mild and pleasant, almost springlike except that the smell of the leaves was crisp instead of new and nascent.

As for disturbing Miller in the middle of the night, Miller

himself had told him about desperate emergencies in the wee hours of the morning, when children had been sent running from shacks an hour or two away. This was no emergency, not a physical one, anyway, but it was an urgent one to Morton and he didn't know when else he would be able to ask Miller's advice.

Crickets and night birds filled the cool air over the sound of his shoes on the hard dirt road. The rising moon was his only key to the time passing as he turned off the main road onto smaller and smaller byways, until he was sure he was close to Miller's house. He came up a steep rise onto the top of a hill and looked down into the moonlit valley and saw a small house with a shed for a mule. It was bright enough and his eyes were used to the dark to the point where he could recognize Miller's wagon by the side of the shed. To his surprise, a light was on inside, faint, like a kerosene lamp or a candle. Morton hurried down the hill. He had no doubt he was in the right place. Even the white people in this part of the county lived in comparable poverty to the blacks. This house was solid, not tarred together. The garden, even in the dark, was neatly divided, probably into corn, beans, and squash. There was no sign of squalor. It didn't surprise Morton that Miller lived all the way out here without neighbors. White folks were jealous, from what he'd heard in the bar, and the only thing that kept Miller from harassment was that he treated anyone who needed it for no cost except barter, and sometimes not even that. Probably the seeds for the garden, the roof for the house, the mule and cart themselves had come as payment for a difficult childbirth, or a difficult death.

There was a dog tied in the yard and the minute it sensed

him it started to bark. The light in the window disappeared and reappeared at the front door—Miller, in a nightshirt. He opened the screen and came out to quiet the dog and saw Morton.

"Why, young sir," he said without a shred of surprise, "what's wrong?"

Perhaps he expected Morton to tell him that Samuels had cut off another finger, but there was a white doctor for that. Morton stopped in the yard. His questions, the letter he needed to write, his cousins' demands seemed to evaporate. He realized he wasn't sure why he was here except that he was homesick.

Miller held the lamp up so the light made a wider circle. "Are you hurt?"

"No," said Morton, "no. I needed to ask you a question. I'm sorry to bother you so late. I wasn't thinking. I just wasn't sure when I would see you."

"Come and sit down," said Miller, "since you're here." He stepped back to indicate the chairs on the front porch. "Keep your voice down, though. The children are sleeping."

Morton sat, and then Miller sat. He put the lantern on a third chair. Its glow was both homey and ghostly. There were a number of chairs of all different sizes, for children, adults, visitors. There was a table made of planks with a vase of flowers on it as though the family sat outside to eat when the weather was nice. The flowers made Morton even more homesick.

"I think I have to leave," he said, though it was the last thing he had intended to say. "My cousins say I owe them money." He took a breath, afraid he would start to cry. "I need to write my father a letter. I need to ask him to send me the money to get back to Boston." He took another breath. "I'm sorry to bother you so late."

Miller folded his hands together. "Will your father send the money?"

"I don't know. I don't know if he has any to spare."

"You'll have to write a convincing letter, then," said Miller. "If he had the money to send you out here, don't you think he would have kept a little to get you back?"

"I don't know," said Morton, frightened by his own honesty. "Maybe he wanted me gone forever. I was a bad son. I was an extra son. I caused trouble for him."

"What would you do if you went back?"

"I'd work for him, no questions, no payment. I'd be a man for him, not a boy anymore."

"You'd stop thieving," said Miller. "You'd be responsible."

"I would."

"What if he had no work for you?" said Miller. "What if this is his best option, you staying down here, working for the butcher? Would you stay?"

Morton looked off into the dark. "I don't want to stay."

"Could you get back to Boston on what you have?"

"I don't think so."

"Well, young sir," said Miller. "You came here for advice. Let me give you mine. First, you have a job here. Second, if you want to go back to Boston, you have two ways of doing it. Write your father a convincing letter, tell him how you've grown, that you have a trade now—he wouldn't have to find work for you if he has none for himself. Third, you can stay here until you have enough money to get yourself back home."

"But my cousins say I owe them more than I have—more than I can earn in a year."

"Your cousins are lying," said Miller blandly. "People know them. I know them. And even if they weren't lying, you wouldn't have to pay them today or tomorrow. You pay them after you ask your father if you should. They have to respect that. Anyone would."

There was a sound behind the screen door. It opened and Miller's little son stepped into the faint light at the edge of the kerosene lamp.

"Go back to bed, Henry," said Miller. "Everything's all right."

Instead Henry came and crawled into his father's lap. His eyes were luminous, not sleepy at all. Morton half expected him to put his thumb in his mouth and curl up like a much younger child, but he didn't. He just watched Morton, unblinking, without comprehension.

Miller stroked the boy's hair. "There's no such thing as an extra son," he said. "Unless your father has said that to your face, there's no reason to think it. These are hard times. We have to value what we have, even if we have to send it away." He was silent for a while. "In my family line, the sons didn't become doctors. They were laborers until I came along, and slaves before that. People seem to think I have something to bequeath, but I don't." He touched his son's face. "Henry will be whatever he'll be. If it's labor he's suited for, then so it is. And you," he said to Morton, "if it's your way to become a butcher and work for Samuels, and not go home for a few years, then so it is. It's respectable work. You don't shame anyone by doing it. You have a place to live and you're fed. One day these hard times will be behind us and you'll be able to go back home on your own. You'll have a skill and some money in your pocket. None of those are bad things. And homesickness," he added, "should pass. And I say that as a doctor."

Morton let himself smile.

"Write to your father," said Miller. "Tell him everything, but let him know you're doing well. If he thinks it's time for you to come back, he'll let you know. You don't need to sound desperate. You aren't. You understand?"

Morton nodded.

"Well, then," said Miller. "You have a long walk back and an early start in the morning, I'm sure." He stood up slowly and Henry slid to his feet. Miller held one of his son's hands as the boy rubbed his eyes. "Goodnight, young sir."

"Thank you," said Morton. "Goodnight."

In the morning, at the butcher's there was no talk of Morton's cousins. The only unusual thing was that Emma came out from the house to bring him a cup of coffee and sat down to talk with him about this and that. Before she went back in, she laughed at something he said and touched his shoulder.

In the evening he started the letter home again. This time he said,

Dear Father,
I am doing surprisingly well.

Goat Island

MY COUSIN, RJ, picked me up at the bus station in Truth or Consequences, in southern New Mexico, and drove me the short five miles to the tiny town of Elephant Butte, where he lived with his father, Roy. When I'd told my friends back in Baltimore where I was going, the ones who were potters, like me, nodded approvingly because of the reputation of the New Mexican clay. My other friends said, *Ellie, are those real places?*

This was the *Butt* end of the state, as RJ always said, and I was waiting for him to say it as we came around the dam-end of Elephant Butte lake. He didn't. He wasn't saying much, which was unlike him. Even when I said, "So, how's your dad?" he just drove faster on the turns. I tightened my seatbelt and hugged my backpack to my chest. RJ was a moody guy to begin with, but four years of fighting in the Gulf had made him worse.

We came down out of the sparse hills and past the spillway where tourists parked for the best view of the Elephant Butte, an island which looked more or less like a standing elephant. Normally the Butte was surrounded by a forty-square-mile lake of dammed Rio Grande, which was in turn surrounded by hundreds of miles of sand and cactus. On my last visit, a year and a half ago, I'd watched from the Greyhound window as fishermen from Albuquerque hauled their powerboats into the desert for the weekend. The lake had been high and blue then, the elephant festooned with sage brush, with more of a woolly mammoth look to it. Now it was stripped to dirt and rocks. Instead of reflecting in the water, it cast a shadow over shallow murk. The water was so low, a sandbar connected the elephant to the shoreline. It wasn't even an island anymore.

"What the hell?" I said.

"Drought," said RJ. "The desert's going back to being a desert."

"What about the goats?" There had been goats living on the Elephant, trapped there actually, while it was an island. The reservoir was part of a state park and the rangers fed them.

"They were stupid," said RJ. "They left as soon as they got a chance."

I looked in the other direction. Sagebrush and prickly pear cactus. Not a goat in sight. "Can they survive out there?"

"The coyotes probably got 'em. If they had any sense, they would have stayed on that damn rock."

"Poor goats." I looked back at what was left of the lake. Roy and RJ used to fish on it. They'd had a bass boat called the *Big Deal*. When I came down to visit, we'd putter around the edges of the lake while Roy, between drags on his cigarette, would tell me how cheap it was to live in the middle of nowhere. He'd say, "You should get your ass down here permanent, girl!" It was RJ who'd convinced me to move, though, when he'd driven me through the hot streets of Truth or Consequences and pointed out the dusty storefront studios of the local potters who lived and worked and pursued their artistic dreams without a lot of overhead.

Now RJ turned off the main road into a neighborhood of trailers and one-story houses. Most of the driveways were empty. The chain-link fences that surrounded every single house were padlocked. From the sharp, dark mountains in the west, clouds full of snow rushed overhead.

The Roys, as my mother referred to them, lived at the end of a dirt road exotically named Al Hambra. RJ steered through their chain-link gate and stopped in the gravel drive in front of Roy's tan-colored house. Cactus clustered along their fence. Tinsel left over from Christmas glittered in the stunted pine trees. The first thing I noticed was that the boat, the *Big Deal*, was missing.

"Where's the boat?" I asked.

"Sold it," said RJ. "Medical bills." He opened the car door. The wind tried to slam it shut again and he held it open with his foot. He turned to me, his face tight. It struck me again, how looking at him was almost like looking in a mirror. Rough reddish hair. The pale but somehow ruddy Scots-Irish complexion. We were more like brother and sister instead of cousins.

"Dad's not good," said RJ. "Remember how your dad was?"

My father had died three years ago from lymphatic cancer, which my doctor mother had been powerless to stop, and which had consumed him right before our eyes. Roy'd been diagnosed with emphysema in November. Now, in January, the doctors were telling him that his heart was a mess. When RJ'd told me, over the phone, I'd almost decided not to make the trip.

"You don't need the extra trouble," I'd said.

"Come anyway," he'd said. "He needs the company."

Now I said, "He's that bad?"

RJ gave the door an angry kick to keep it open. "I'll help you with your stuff."

SHERRY LONG was inside with Roy. Sherry lived next door in a cinderblock house that Buddy, her late husband, had built in the seasons between fishing. I'd never met Buddy, who'd had a heart attack and gone off the road while he was towing a boat. His truck slammed into an embankment and then the boat rammed the cab from behind. His body was so mangled that Sherry'd had him cremated. She'd told me all of this on the first day I met her, three years ago, when she gave me a tour of her house. Buddy was represented by carefully arranged little shrines of old bill-caps, hand-tied flies, snapshots and trophies with accompanying newspaper photos. One showed him with an immense walleye he'd caught when they'd lived in Minnesota. Buddy was overweight and happy. The fish was huge and made me think of some kind of dinosaur. It hung by its tail, as long as Buddy was tall.

Sherry always arrived with food. Today the Roys' house smelled of cookies and there was a pecan pie on the kitchen counter. Sherry popped up from of her chair when she saw me and threw her arms around my neck. "Ellie! You look so thin!" Which meant I would be required to eat cookies and pie. She pulled me over to the table where Roy sat, dressed in an undershirt and sweatpants, tethered to his oxygen. When RJ had said *that bad*, I'd been afraid he'd be thin and sick-looking, but at first glance he hadn't changed. He was still a big man, just like my dad. Roy'd been a Marine in the seventies, a mechanic on the NASCAR circuit in the eighties, and made a living fixing lawnmowers and snowmobiles in North Dakota before retiring to the warmer, cheaper climes of southern New Mexico. He'd weighed three hundred pounds the first time I'd come to visit and told me he'd taken up smoking to lose weight. He didn't seem any different until I gave him a kiss. Before, he'd always kissed me on the lips.

"Germs," he said, and we kissed each other's cheeks. He adjusted the clear plastic tubing of his oxygen where the cannula looped around his ears and under his nostrils.

Sherry held out the plate of cookies. "Raisin oatmeal," she said and got up to cut me a piece of pie.

"Let the girl put her shit in the bedroom before you start stuffing her," said Roy and pointed at the door to his room.

The last time I'd been here, I'd slept in their camper. It was gone, I now realized, gone the way of the *Big Deal.*

"What're you waitin' for?" said Roy. "Can't you see Sherry wants your opinion on the pie?"

"Where're you sleeping?" I said.

Roy jerked a thumb toward his battered leather recliner.

"Can't lay flat no more," he said. "You're takin' the bed."

I glanced at RJ, who gave me the slightest of nods.

"Okay." I dragged my backpack and duffel into his bedroom.

Roy's king-sized bed filled the room. His wooden dresser barely fit into one corner. The only window looked out onto the carport. The last time I'd been here, sleeping in the camper, I'd woken up when coyotes came down the road in the middle of the night. I'd had a good view from the camper, and the coyotes, skinny, unconcerned shadows in full moonlight, trotted through the neighborhood, not making a sound themselves but bringing out the false bravado of every dog for miles. Now, through the miniblinds, I had a narrow view of the driveway, the fence, and the cactus hedge.

I dropped my pack on the bed and dug for the presents I'd brought. One was a card from my mom. The other was a pot I'd made. I unwrapped it from its newspaper cocoon. It was just a little pot with an earthy green glaze and a clean-fitting lid. The glaze had interesting horizontal flaws that made the pot look like it was painted with an imaginary landscape. I should've brought a couple of my coffee mugs. The Roys would have used coffee mugs, but I hated coffee mugs. I loved this pot. The Roys wouldn't have a clue what to do with it. It wasn't a sugar bowl. It wasn't big enough for candy. It was just a tiny pot, light and good to hold. It would collect dust on a shelf until Roy died. Then RJ would pack it, move, and forget about it, but I wouldn't have considered giving them the pot if I hadn't loved it so much. I re-wrapped it and brought it out to the kitchen.

"Here." I gave Roy the card from my mother. "My mom sent this."

He opened it and read the card and pushed it to the middle of the table. "I'll call your ma tonight."

"She won't be home till late."

"She out drinkin'?" said Roy.

My mother was phone-banking for public television this week. When she drank, she drank moderately-priced French vintages. Roy knew that. "Yeah," I said. "She'll be partying all night. You can try her tomorrow afternoon when her hangover wears off."

RJ snickered. "What's the matter with your family?"

"It's worse than you think," I said. "I brought pot."

RJ let out a snort of a laugh. Roy unwrapped the newspaper and held up the pot, squinting at it. It looked microscopic in his hands.

"It's a beautiful color," said Sherry. "Roy, don't you think it's a beautiful color?"

"It's nice," said Roy. "Nice and...green. We'll put something in it. Like...I don't know." He showed it to RJ. "What can we put in it?"

"A grape," said RJ.

"You don't have to put anything in it," I said.

Roy took the lid off and put it on. "You makin' money with these things?"

"The big bucks are in coffee mugs."

Sherry nodded. "You should see some of the coffee mugs they sell up there in Santa Fe. You should see the prices."

Roy adjusted his cannula, turned the pot around a couple of times. "We'll put it on the windowsill." He gave it to RJ, who dutifully took it to the kitchen window and put it on the sill next to a coleus growing in a pink plastic bowl. Soon my little pot would be obscured by green leaves streaked with yellow veins. There were worse things.

SHERRY LEFT to go to Truth or Consequences, which everyone called T or C, where she volunteered at the thrift shop in the senior center. Roy stretched and yawned and said he needed a nap. RJ and I left him at the end of his oxygen tether, in his recliner in the living room with the TV on.

Outside the wind plucked at RJ's shirt. The shirt was

newish, light blue with pearly plastic buttons. I thought he'd dressed up to come get me, but he said it was something Sherry had picked out and given to him.

"Sherry comes over every day?" I said.

"Just about. She'd bring over dinner every night if we let her." I thought we were going to walk around the neighborhood, but RJ got back in the car. "Come on."

I got in too. "Where're we going?"

"Back to the Butte," said RJ.

He drove and I admired the scenery aloud. RJ rolled his eyes but pulled off where I had a good view of the remains of the lake. He reached past me to pull a sooty-looking plastic bag and a pack of matches out of the glove compartment. The bag had a joint in it, a big one, about halfway smoked. He groped under his seat and produced a bottle in a paper bag.

Nothing about this shocked me except for the time of day. "Early, isn't it?" I said. "I mean it's, like, one-thirty."

"Yeah, yeah, yeah."

He lit the joint for me. I took a hit and let the smoke out between my teeth. RJ always had a little pot on him, but this was a blunt-sized, good-quality smoke.

"How can you afford weed like this?" I said. "Did you get a job or something?"

He laughed. "I have friends who give me a discount."

"Good to have those kinds of friends."

"Yeah."

"So what does the doctor say?" I took another hit and held it.

RJ swigged from the paper bag. "She says he could last for years."

"That's good, right?"

"I guess. Sherry introduced him to all her friends with emphysema and heart trouble. There's a couple not too far from here. Dennis and Edna. They're both on oxygen. He's got forty percent lung capacity. She's got something like sixty-five."

"So they manage to get around."

"Sure," said RJ. "Hell, Edna still smokes."

I hacked out my toke. "With oxygen in the house? She'll blow herself up."

RJ shrugged. "Maybe she doesn't want to die of emphysema." Another swig. "Dad was really bad about it when he was diagnosed. I'd get up to piss in the middle of the night and he'd be in the living room, just bawlin'. You know, trying to be quiet about it."

"What did you do?"

"What was I supposed to do? Tell him everything's going to be all right?" He took another swallow. "I told his doctor. She put him on antidepressants."

"Do they help?"

"Well," said RJ, "I used to be afraid to let him go out driving by himself. Now he doesn't want to go anywhere. Just sits around."

I pondered this, pondered the shrinking lake, the missing goats. When had they decided to escape, I wondered. Had they waited for every puddle to disappear? How did goats make those kinds of decisions, anyway? Was there a lead goat, or was it some kind of herd consensus?

We smoked until the joint was gone.

"Is there anything I can do?" I said.

"He likes you," said RJ. "Just stick around."

WE CALLED my mom that night—nine in New Mexico, eleven in Maryland. Roy talked to her first, jovial and brother-in-law-like. "Yeah, she's here," he said, "she looks awfully skinny though. Ain't you feedin' her?" A long pause while my mother probably went on and on about how her only child had left her all alone. Then she must have asked Roy how he was. His tone didn't really change, but he hunched his shoulders and leaned over the table. "They got me on oxygen 24/7 now. These damn doctors don't know what the hell they're doing. No offense." Another pause. "Yeah, the boy's hangin' in there, helping me out when he's not sittin' around on his ass. Here." He pushed the phone at RJ, who grinned boyishly and said, "Hi, Aunt Deborah," exactly the way I remembered him saying it when he was a little kid. Finally RJ gave the phone to me.

"Ellie," said my mother from the hot earpiece, "how was your trip?"

"It was long," I said.

"Did they even give you a meal? The last time I flew, all we got were peanuts."

"We got pretzels and soda."

"Flying is awful these days."

"It really is."

Silence on her end. Maybe she felt like yelling at me, but she never yelled. My dad's family was better at it by far. My mom was usually very careful about the things she allowed herself to say. "Listen," she said, "I know you don't want me to interfere, but I just want to say, the sooner you have a job and a place of your own, the easier it'll be for everyone."

"Okay, Mom." What she hadn't said, but what she always said about my cousin and my uncle, was that *They're never going to be able to help you. They can't even help themselves.*

"They aren't rich, Ellie," my mother said. "They'll share whatever they have, but you can't take advantage of that. If you need money, I'll send you money."

I'd saved my own money so that she couldn't tell me what to do with it. I didn't want to make her angrier by telling her that.

"Okay," I said. "Thanks."

"Roy sounds terrible. How does he look? No, don't tell me. Call me some other time. We'll talk."

"Okay, Mom."

"I love you, Ellie."

"Love you, Mom."

FOR DINNER that night, we had chicken fingers and Minute Rice. RJ had a lite beer and so did I. Roy had herbal tea. We all had a salad made with iceberg lettuce that had lost its crispness. Roy ate his with the air of someone who has to take their medicine. We ate more of the pecan pie, which was exceptional. All the while, the TV ran in the background, just visible from where I was sitting. News and weather. Entertainment Tonight. The Friday night lineup. We moved to the living room and watched a John Wayne movie. Roy fell asleep in his recliner. RJ snored on the sofa. I brushed my teeth and crawled into the immense landscape of Roy's bed.

That night I discovered that the problem with my staying at the Roys wasn't going to be that I was imposing on them, or that they couldn't afford me as a long-term guest. It was the snoring. It was loud, and persistent. It was the kind of snoring that resonated through the floor and the bedsprings, no matter how many pillows I put over or under my head. RJ sounded like a chain saw. Roy sounded like he was suffocating, which he was, which made it worse. This hadn't been a problem when I'd been sleeping in the trailer, and as I lay there and listened to it, I wondered if I should just go outside and curl up in the back of RJ's car. But it was cold out there, and the roach, which would have knocked me out, was all smoked up. I wondered what to do. Then I turned over and wondered what to do. An artist friend with terrible insomnia had made a painting he called "The Palace at 2 AM"—an abstract building with different doors to different rooms painted with scenes of the things he couldn't shake out of his mind in the wee hours. My palace solidified around 1:30 with the last conversation I'd had with my mother in Baltimore.

She'd knocked on the door to my dismal apartment and told me she was there to help me pack, which of course wasn't true. I was wrapping plates in newspaper and stuffing them into a Beefeater Gin box. It was mid-January, which in Baltimore meant a depressing combination of sleet, rain, and short, dark days. Outside, wet ice clung to the fire escape and dripped into the trashy alley below. On days like this I would have thrown myself off the roof for a glimpse of blue sky.

My mother held up a mug I'd made and kept for myself—pretty blues with darker accents along the lip and handle. "This is beautiful," she said. "Why don't you try to get into one of those galleries downtown? You could make some real money."

Every time we had this conversation, I felt like crying. I

was grinding out mugs in twenty square feet of rented space while my ceramics friends from art college went to grad school making incredible, magical things and lining up galleries to show them in. My grad school experience boiled down to not getting into one. Coffee mugs sucked up the time and space and energy I needed to articulate in mud what my professors had called "interior statements." I wasn't even sure what my interior statements were at this point.

"I don't want to make mugs," I said.

My mom crushed newspaper around two water glasses I'd gotten from Goodwill and which I'd meant to throw in recycling. I could see how angry she was by how carefully she packed my worthless glassware. I could tell she wanted to offer me things, like money for a nicer apartment, a car. She'd offered before as I'd sobbed over my grad school rejections. She'd gently, gently suggested I go back to school for a bachelor's in something else, and I'd yelled at her about *art,* and how long it took to be really *good,* and how grad school had *nothing* to do with it.

"When's your plane?" she said.

"Thursday. At two-thirty."

"Why didn't you make it for after five? I can't take you. I'll be at work."

"I know," I said.

"Who's going to take you?"

"The train goes to the airport from downtown. It's easy."

She looked away from me. I tucked in the flaps of the Beefeater box and waited for her to finish with the tape. Friends were coming to take away everything I owned, except for what would fit into a backpack. Mom wanted me to put it all in her basement, but that was too much like agreeing to move back home one day. She gave me the tape and sat at my kitchen table. I forced the Beefeater box closed. It was pretty much the last thing.

My mom looked around the apartment, at the bed and the crummy sofa. "What're you going to do with the furniture?"

"Friends are coming for it tomorrow."

"Tomorrow's Wednesday," she said. "Where're you going to sleep?"

"They're not taking the bed until Thursday."

"Why don't they just come for everything on Thursday?"

"I don't know, Mom. That's just the way they wanted to do it."

She pushed her hair back from her face. I would have asked how her own mother had reacted when she'd finally left home for good, but Mom was just finishing medical school when she was my age. Her parents couldn't have been prouder when she got a job in Baltimore and moved there from upstate New York.

"Oh, Ellie," she said.

I STARED at the ceiling of Roy's bedroom and listened to the snoring. I went out to the kitchen and groped around until I found the fifth of Jack Daniels that I knew RJ kept hidden behind the cereal boxes. I took a big, fiery swallow and went back to bed. After a while the snoring paused for distant, melancholy howls outside. There was a moment of breathless, blessed silence, and I fell asleep.

THE NEXT MORNING Roy took a nap after breakfast. RJ retreated into the bathroom with the local paper. I went out for a walk and saw a little black and white dog rolling in the dust in Sherry's yard. Sherry took in all kinds of animals. She fed people who couldn't feed themselves. Either she had a new dog or she had company.

I stood in the road by Sherry's gate, conflicted. It was a beautiful, if windy morning, and it would be nice to clear the sleeplessness out of my head by briskly striding around the neighborhood, but I dawdled by the gate. If Sherry happened to glance past her flowery kitchen curtains and saw me standing here, I'd be in her house for at least an hour, eating and listening to what was going on at the senior center.

I felt like I didn't have time for that. I was supposed to be out looking for a way to pursue my hopes and dreams of becoming a successful potter without resorting to coffee mugs.

The dog came up to the fence and wagged his tail at me. I decided the hopes and dreams could wait, opened the gate and went in. I knocked on the screen door.

Sherry pushed it open, with a spatula in one hand and a plate of pancakes in the other. In the kitchen, I could see a skinny, elderly man, carefully pouring syrup. Everything smelled buttery.

"Ellie!" said Sherry, "Come on in! Meet Ed." She set the plate down in front of an empty chair before I could tell her I'd eaten already. Ed stuck out his hand for me to shake. Ed was thin and cancerous, with the air of a life-long smoker. His eyes, which might have been a pale blue once, were filmy now.

"Is that your dog out there?" I asked.

"Oh yeah," said Ed. "He has to stay out because of Sherry's cats."

"You have cats now?" I said to Sherry.

She pointed toward the bedroom. "There they are."

In the shadows, two cats sat just inside the doorway, both black. Only one had a full set of ears.

Sherry poured Ed more coffee. "Ellie's staying with Roy. She's a potter. She's going to find a place and set up her own studio. Isn't that right, Ellie?"

I nodded and took a bite of pancake. The pancakes were perfect, with lovely brown surfaces and cream-colored sides. Everything Sherry cooked was made with Betty Crocker precision.

"There's a potter guy down in T or C," said Ed. "You been down there? He helped me change a tire on my truck once. Maybe he'd hire you on."

"I'll check," I said, but I knew who he was talking about and I knew the answer was no. His name was Larry and he was a one-man operation on a "my-wife-works-at-Wal-Mart" budget. The last time I was here I'd lurked in his studio for a couple of hours talking about being a potter in Baltimore. Larry was professionally friendly and that was all.

"He's in the paper today," said Sherry, and pulled out the "Local Color" section.

She showed me the photo on the front page. It was Larry, standing in front of his shop, holding an exquisitely delicate container that vaguely resembled a soup tureen. It was glazed in three variations of turquoise and was far too fragile-looking to ever put soup in. I remembered his work as being sturdily functional, serviceable stuff that anyone could buy and use and appreciate on some level—like coffee mugs. But this was different. This was art. The headline said, "Local Potter Shows in Santa Fe Gallery."

"Damn," I said.

"Bet he's makin' some money now," said Ed, sipping coffee.

I took the paper and started reading the article. Years of hard work, living on a budget, and finally, a stroke of luck—or inspiration—that landed him in a gallery up north. I looked at the tureen again, and Larry smiling next to it. Was this his "interior statement?"

"You thinking about buying a place?" said Sherry. "You want to set yourself up, like him?"

"Well," I said.

"Hell, there's a trailer down the street for sale," Ed interrupted. "They can't want too much for it. It's a piece of crap, but you could work out of it and go back to Roy's for a shower."

Sherry raised an eyebrow. I couldn't tell if she approved or not.

"Where is it?" I said.

"Round the corner," said Sherry, pointing vaguely. "It's a pretty kind of blue."

There was a sound from the hallway and I glanced at the cats, who'd come a step closer. The one with ears let out a raspy meow.

"What happened to the other one?" I said.

Sherry shook her head. "Who knows. They were both strays. People just dump their animals around here. They just leave 'em."

"Which one's blind?" said Ed.

"The one with ears," said Sherry. "I call 'im Blackie. The other one can't hear. It don't matter what you call 'im."

AFTER THE PANCAKES I walked around the Al Hambra neighborhood looking for the trailer and found it right away. It sat on a bare little lot with a fence and a scruffy cactus. There was no For Sale sign, so maybe Ed was wrong, but I stared at it anyway, imagining a brick kiln in the back and rows of pots on wooden shelves. I wouldn't be too far from the Roys but not too close either. I peered around to see if their place was visible from any angle. It wasn't. I went back and asked Roy about the trailer.

"You don't want that thing," said Roy. He and RJ were at the table sharing a bag of Cheetos. "It's a piece of shit. Always had problems with the septic."

"But I could just use it for studio space."

"Piece of shit," repeated Roy. "Damn thing'll blow away in the next big wind."

THE NEXT MORNING, I got up before anyone else. It'd been another noisy, exhausting night. I sat hunched over my bowl of cornflakes, eating as quietly as possible as Ray sprawled in his recliner, sound asleep. I watched the birds come to the feeder RJ had put up for Roy's entertainment as he sat, roped to his oxygen.

One bird looked remarkably like a cardinal, but creamy underneath. One looked like a mockingbird, but twice the size. The crows, who didn't come to the feeder but flew purposefully overhead, were different, too. They had slender bodies and narrow wings. They still seemed to travel in threes, though, like the ones back east. My mother had pointed that out to me.

"There're always three," she'd said. "The mother, the father, and one from the last nest who stays to help with next year's chicks."

"How do you know that?" I'd said. "You're making that up."

She'd given me this look. "Your father told me." It'd been almost a year since he'd died.

I went outside to the gate, out in the cold morning air, to find the newspaper, which got thrown over the fence in some pre-dawn hour. I sat at the picnic table under the carport, relishing the quiet, and searched the real estate ads for anything that might work out as studio space. Unused boathouses or garages—anything with some ground, electricity, running water and shade. There wasn't much. Mostly lake-front "bargains" for boaters, some three-bedroom houses for thousands of dollars near the unlikely golf course. There were a dozen trailer homes, which sounded trashy and were still outside my zone of affordability. I read the front section, which was mostly about crimes committed by people from Mexico, or who at least *looked* like people from Mexico. I must've been fairly absorbed, because the Roys had been yelling at each other, inside the house, for some time before I actually noticed it.

Wind chimes tinkled under the carport. I turned around to look at the mountains to the west, covered with snow. I couldn't hear exactly what they were yelling about, but there were breaks when RJ would let Roy get his two cents in, then

RJ again. I smoothed my hair against the wind. Every once in a while, my father would yell at my mother. It sounded like the Roys did now. She never yelled back. She held her ground without raising her voice. My mom was quiet and precise and composed. My dad was emotional and loud, and he'd told me once in a resigned tone that he hoped I'd be able to solve problems like my mother did. When they fought, he'd leave the house and come back with a video, usually a cowboy movie. She'd make spaghetti and meatballs for dinner. We'd watch TV in silence, and that would be it. They rarely fought, I realized after my dad died, because he'd never figured out how to win.

I sat at the table a while longer.

The yelling went on.

I could go over to Sherry's and have pancakes with her and Ed. I could call before I came back to the Roys, using some excuse, like, *are we out of cookies?* Or I could go for a walk. The lake wasn't far. I'd come back through town and stop by the grocery store. I'd make spaghetti and meatballs for dinner. By evening everything would be fine. I struck off down Al Hambra, heading for the park.

On the way, I passed the piece-of-shit turquoise trailer. Now a For Sale sign leaned against the fence, not even stuck in the ground yet. The signpost had a plastic box attached to it for "for sale" fliers, but that was empty. I walked briskly by, trying not to think about how I could never afford what I needed for myself out here, so far from my family and still so uncomfortably close.

ABOUT A MILE from the park, there was a pull-off by the side of the road for those who wanted to stop and admire the drought-stricken lake, the Elephant Butte, and the sandbar where the goats had made their exit. I turned the other way to look at the mountains, topped with snow. There was nothing man-made between me and the mountains—just dark dots of brush—and the lack of scale made the distance strange, like the mountains were a hundred miles away, or fifty, or maybe five. It was impossible to tell.

I turned back to the lake. From this angle, it was starkly obvious how much the lake had shrunk. The water was so low that the concrete boat ramps, which had been extended further and further as the drought went on, seemed like streams of asphalt running into the water. The shoreline, which had been a long, sloping beach, was now a loose, rocky drop-off, like the side of a mesa. Anything with enough weight could come loose and roll down into the water. Trailers and mobile homes and cars. Even the picnic shelters, which had been at the water's edge a couple of years ago, were at least a quarter mile from the beach. From the pull-off, I had a good view of the town of Elephant Butte and Truth or Consequences just beyond. From here it seemed like the land itself tilted in this direction and before long everything might just slip into this damned-up puddle. It struck me that RJ was right. There was no drought. This was just a correction.

I took a couple of steps down the hill thinking I would walk down to the elephant and see what the goats had left behind when I heard a car turn in at the pull-off. I looked back expecting out-of-season tourists, but it was RJ.

"Hey," I said in surprise as he got out.

"Hey," he said. He had a bottle with him in a paper bag. "Where're you going?"

I pointed.

"The Butte?" he hauled himself out of the car and stood unsteadily. "Great. Can I come?"

He was already snockered. "What the hell," I said. "I mean, sure."

We walked through the sage and prickly pear, out to the edge of the lake where the cactus and weeds ended abruptly. The sandbar wasn't as solid as it had looked from the pull-off. We waded through the soggy sand until we got to the first broad stones leading to the island. RJ waltzed along with remarkable grace, which made me wonder about the length and breadth of his drinking.

RJ was two years older than me. When I was little, my parents would pack up and drive down to Houston where my Aunt Katie lived, for a week-long Fourth of July get-together with my dad's big ol' family. There was Uncle Roy, their other sister, Aunt Lucy, dozens of cousins and a raft of distant relations. There were so many kids that we were basically unsupervised. I remember RJ setting off bottle rockets when he couldn't have been more than eight. Once when he choked on a hotdog, I remember Roy putting down his beer to smack him so hard on the back that RJ fell face down on the concrete and came up with blood all over his face. Roy, drunk off his ass, laughed.

My mother and I took RJ to the bathroom to clean him up. My mom looked him over for older, abusive bruises, but she didn't find any.

There was a lot of drinking, and there was the inevitable point where my father and his brother would end up shouting at each other. The last summer we went, I was nine. Everything started normally, but by sundown, the drinking and shouting had turned into swearing and punches. My dad needed six stitches over his left eye, and after that my mother refused to go to Texas ever again.

My first adolescent memory of RJ was when I was fifteen and my dad got a phone call from Roy. It went something like this:

"He did what? The police picked him up? They can't search his car without...no shit. Was it his?" Long, listening silence during which my dad scratched at his Saturday morning stubble. Then: "You need help with bail? Hell, Roy, when we were his age we were assholes too. You remember what dad did with you? Yep. Yep. It straightened you right out." My dad hung up and turned to me. "Guess RJ's going into the Marines."

"Not to pry," I said to him now, "but are you not working because you're drinking too much, or are you drinking too much because you're not working?"

He laughed and took another swig. "You were listening."

"To what?"

"Me and Dad. Screaming at each other."

"Not really."

"Well," said RJ, "that's what we always scream at each other about."

"So which is it?"

RJ shrugged. "Hell, I'm taking care of him. When do I have time to work?"

"He wasn't always this sick."

"He is now." He tilted the bottle all the way back and swallowed. "He gets tired of me being in the house all the time. And then he's afraid to let me leave. It kinda goes in cycles." He screwed the lid on the bottle and put it down carefully, between the dry rocks.

We walked on without saying much else. The closer we got to the elephant, the more of the blackish clay strata I could see in the part that had been submerged when the lake was high. There was a thick, gooey-grayish streak running around the entire elephant, like a ring in a bathtub.

"Huh," I said.

RJ belched. "Huh what?"

"Clay," I said and showed him the band. "There's tons of it." I pointed to the same dark line in the big hills behind the rooftops of Elephant Butte. "There's more. It's all over the place."

"Obviously," said RJ. "The Indians have been making shit out of it for, like, a hundred million years."

We'd come to the foot of the elephant, but there was no apparent upward path. The rock went straight up to a small flat ridge. Maybe the goats looked down from there at this slowly emerging strip, making whatever plans goats are capable of.

I squatted down to have a look at the clay deposit and scraped out a chunk. I dipped the chunk in the water and mashed it with both hands until it was soft. RJ hunkered down beside me. I made a little goat, tiny, lumpy, ugly. I handed it to him.

He turned it over. "It's nice."

I wiped my hands on my jeans and stood.

RJ stood, too, hunched his shoulders against the wind and scuffed the dirt. He held the goat carefully, like I'd made something magical, precious. "So you just dig up the clay and make stuff out of it? That seems too easy."

"I'd have to mix it with some other things," I said. "I'd have to experiment with it."

"Don't you have to do something with fire?"

"You dig a pit and fill it up with wood. You put in the pots and cover it up and let it burn."

RJ looked around at the treeless landscape. "You'd have to buy wood."

"I can use pretty much anything that burns. It doesn't have to be wood." Dry cactus or tumbleweed. Newspaper. Charcoal. Clay wasn't picky.

RJ placed the goat carefully on the ground, wiped his hands and put them in his pockets. "People move in and out of here all the time. You could find a secondhand trailer. I could help you fix it up. Obviously you'll need some money."

"Obviously I have some," I said. "I've got about fifteen hundred bucks."

He frowned. "Your mom gave you fifteen hundred bucks?"

"No, idiot," I said. "I earned it. Making fucking coffee mugs."

He blinked, like I might start yelling at him, like his dad.

"Sorry," I said. "You're not an idiot."

He gave me a brief, boozy smile. He gestured at the desert behind the elephant. "You should find someplace in town. You sure don't want to be out there all by yourself."

I smiled. "You want to move into my secondhand trailer with me?"

"I was talking about a dog," said RJ.

"That seems too easy," I said.

"Maybe it is," said RJ. He took his hands out of his pockets and pointed me back toward the car. "Come on. I want you to meet some friends of mine."

We drove into the dry hills east of Elephant Butte, down a two-lane highway that followed a healthy-looking tributary of the Rio Grande. It was cold, but unusually sunny for this time of year, and the hard light made the landscape flat and chalky. RJ focused on driving while intoxicated and grunted instead of making conversation, which left me wishing I'd taken his keys. I looked out the window at the river, the hills, the flat blue sky. We came around a turn and the sun flashed on the surface of the river, which for some reason made me look up. Overhead, hawks were circling. The sun, at its hard, noonish angle, shone through the feathers of their wings and tails, making them into golden fans. I stared with my mouth open. They were like mythic birds in ancient paintings. They were like something you might never see again, and I watched them until we took the next turn. They disappeared from view but the feeling of portent, which I never got and barely believed in, knotted up in my belly like menstrual cramps.

RJ's friends, Hazel and Harley, lived down a hill at a crook in the river, their house and barn almost hidden by cottonwood trees. We rattled across the cattle-guard and a bunch of dogs raced out of the creek bed, soaked and muddy, followed by three little kids in flip flops. Despite the chill of the day, the kids were as wet and dirty as the dogs, each of them a bright-haired blond, none any older than eight. I couldn't tell if they were boys or girls.

RJ stopped the car for the kids. "Where's your granddad?"

"Harley went to town," said the tallest one. "Hazel's at the house." He, or she, looked at me with frank gray eyes. "Who're you?"

"I'm Ellie. I'm RJ's cousin."

"She's an artist," said RJ. "She makes things out of mud."

"Cool," said the muddy eight-year-old.

"What's your name?" I said.

"Sunny," said the kid. Or maybe it was Sonny.

"Want a ride?" said RJ.

"No thanks," said the kid. "We're excavating." He or she gave me a little wave, and they ran off into the cottonwoods, the dogs bounding after them.

"What a great place to be a kid," I said. "Are they on vacation?"

"Those are Hazel's grandkids," said RJ. "Their mother's in jail for dealing. Hazel's raising them."

The house and barn were on the other side of the creek. I saw a couple of peacocks and a pony through the trees. There were cats everywhere. Hazel was reading the newspaper in a sunny spot on the front porch and got up when she saw us. She didn't look like a grandmother. She didn't look like a relic from the sixties either, as I'd expected. She was a big woman in a T-shirt and jeans, and the newspaper she was reading was entirely in Spanish. RJ introduced me and Hazel invited us into the kitchen for tea and Girl Scout cookies.

"Melissa's in Brownies this year," said Hazel. She shook

out a plateful of Thin Mints. "We're up to our asses in cookies. Want to buy a couple boxes?"

"Sure," said RJ. "Dad loves Thin Mints."

"How's your dad doing?" said Hazel.

"He has good days and bad days." RJ got a mug from the cupboard, poured hot water from a Thermos, and helped himself to a teabag. All the cups on the shelf were handmade. Nice stuff. Stoneware with elegant handles, and some kind of ash glaze.

Hazel saw me examining the mugs. "You like those?"

I nodded. "The glaze is gorgeous."

"Ellie's a potter," said RJ.

Hazel turned her own cup back and forth in her hands. "We used to have a potter here a couple of years ago. Harley let him set up out behind the barn. He turned out to be a mean son-of-a-bitch drunk. He'd run around at night howling and he scared the kids to death. We kicked him out, but he made some nice stuff before he left." She turned to me. "We still have a lot of his shit. You want to see it? Maybe there's something you could use."

I tried not to get my hopes up. "Sure."

"Behind the barn" meant a quarter-mile walk along a trickle of a creek, up a hill covered with prickly pear, and along the edge of a hollow thick with cottonwoods. At the edge of the hollow, away from the trees, was the languishing corpse of a big brick kiln. The only thing that made it something other than a heap of pale yellow firebrick was the stump of its chimney. I walked around it once or twice while everyone watched me like I knew what the hell I was doing.

"What do you think?" said Hazel. "Can you fix it?"

I'd need a lot of new brick. I wondered if Larry, the potter in T or C, would be willing to part with scraps. "Maybe."

"There's more," said Hazel.

At the edge of the cottonwoods, she kicked brush away to reveal a potter's wheel, the foot-powered kind. It was on a level spot not far from the creek, tucked under a shady overhang.

"Try it out," RJ said to me. "See if it works."

I adjusted the seat and sat and gave the wheel a kick. Leaves and sticks flew off. It squeaked and needed a good dose of oil, but it still worked.

"So it's fine?" said Hazel.

I nodded. A dead kiln. An old wheel. It was like picturing myself in the turquoise trailer. Nice idea. Pretty picture. Trouble with the septic.

"What ever happened to this guy?" said RJ.

"Last I heard he was in Mexico, on some beach."

"Making pots?" I said.

"Probably making babies. Here." Hazel led us down into the hollow. What was left of an old trailer sat at an angle in the brush. The roof had rusted through and we could see leggy cactus growing through the floor. Cottonwoods had sprouted in the kitchen sink. An empty vodka bottle sat between curls of cheap veneer on the tiny dining table, as though the potter who'd lived here had just jumped out of his chair and run off in the middle of a bender. Hazel scuffed dead leaves away from broken bits of pottery around the edge of the trailer, some glazed in sultry blues, some still uncolored and earthy.

"He was good," I said.

"He was a drunken shit," said Hazel.

She walked us over to the other side of the trailer where there was a wooden shed with a corrugated metal roof. Hazel yanked the door open. "Can you use any of this stuff?"

Plastic containers of dry chemicals lined the shelves, all labeled in black marker: *feldspar, silica, vermiculite. Cobalt, manganese, rutile.* Fifty-pound sacks of clay powder were stacked neatly against one wall. The floor was covered with firebrick, clean and unused, three or four courses deep, and easily enough to repair the kiln.

"Well?" said Hazel.

I felt almost dizzy. It was a complete shop from what I could see. "How could he leave this here?"

"Because Harley would've shot him if he'd stayed a minute longer," said Hazel. "Can you use it?"

"I don't know if I could pay you what it's worth."

Hazel gave me a funny look. "I didn't ask if you wanted to buy it."

"You can't just give it away."

"Why not?" said Hazel. "It's just junk to me. I'd give you the trailer too it if was fit for anything."

"But what if that guy comes back?"

Hazel snorted.

"Just take it," said RJ. "Say 'yes,' and 'thank you' to the nice lady."

I laughed and felt myself flush. "Yes," I said, "thank you. But I don't have anywhere to put it."

"We'll hang on to it," said Hazel. "You can work here until you get your own place." She turned to RJ. "We got some good stuff for you. Not too many seeds this time."

RJ gave her a big grin and I finally realized this was where he got his pot.

HAZEL AND RJ went back to the house. I checked the chemicals and clay for moisture, but this was the desert. Everything was dry. The metal roof was sound and the bricks had protected everything lying on top of them from any possible ground seep. It was like a time capsule of ceramic equipment. It was mine. I looked in the broken windows of the trailer and scuffed through the leaves and shards. I admired the rejected handles, the paper-thin bodies of broken cups and the disembodied necks of stoneware bottles. One of my professors, whose specialty was ancient Greek ceramics, once brought a box of broken pots to class, each fragment carefully extracted from some historic garbage dump. *Once it's fired,* she said, *clay lasts forever, like glass—it's immortal. No matter how many pieces it breaks into, no matter how deep you bury it, its ugliness or its beauty is forever.* And here she showed us a rim with dents in it, a bit of crooked spout. Embarrassing errors by probably otherwise fine potters. *So be careful what you make,* she said, *and what you throw away—because someday someone's going find it and judge you by your trash.*

I CALLED MY MOTHER that evening when I was sure she'd be home. Roy had fallen asleep in front of the TV. RJ looked like he wanted some personal time with his new stash. I went outside and called from the carport.

My mother never picked up until she knew it wasn't a telemarketer. My own voice answered. *You've reached Doctor Deborah Wage. If this is an emergency, please dial...* I waited past the hospital number and the number for the Children's Clinic until finally there was the beep.

"Mom?" I said, "Mom, it's me. Mom, are you there? Mo-om. It's me-e."

The line clicked. "Oh good. I was getting ready to call you." She sounded tired. "How are you? How's the weather?"

"Windy," I said. "Kind of cold, but not bad. What's it like there?"

"Fine. It's snowing. Well, now it's sleeting. How's Roy doing?"

"Well, you know, he's not any better."

"And?"

"And he's…I don't know…" Bitter wasn't really the right word. Depressed was closer, but not quite right. "I don't know. I mean, in some ways he's just like Dad. There's a big front."

My mother was quiet for a minute. "Do they have him on mood medication?"

"Oh yeah."

"Do you think it's helping?"

"I think it keeps him from crying."

She let out a sigh. My dad's doctors had offered him antidepressants. He'd told them to fuck off. "Your father was scared," she said. "He didn't want you to see it."

"Roy's scared," I said.

"He should be. He's lived his whole life like he was eighteen years old. He thought he was invincible. I'm not saying he deserves this, but my God, what did he expect?"

I tried to decide if she was being fair and realized that on some level, I felt exactly the same way.

How's RJ holding up?" said my mother.

"It's hard to tell. Some days he's right on the ball. And then other times he's…"

"Altered," my mother supplied.

"Well. Yeah."

My mother took a breath. Over the phone it almost sounded like she was taking a drag on a cigarette. "Ellie," she said. "We need to talk to each other like adults now. Not me as a mom, but me as a doctor."

"Okay…"

"Emphysema and heart disease aren't efficient killers," she said. "Roy's overweight and he'll probably develop diabetes before too much longer, but he could live another ten years."

"Ten years?"

"He won't go quickly, like your father. His cancer surprised him. It surprised me. It just came on him like—like—I don't even know what. But Roy's different. He's as mobile as he wants to be, he's functional, and with enough help, he'll be able to make do until the day he goes into the hospital."

"Oh," I said.

"What I'm trying to say," said my mother, "is that Roy can't get better. He can only get worse. It's RJ I want you to think about, and it's yourself. I don't mean to scare you," she said. "I don't mean to say anything bad about RJ. He's a good boy and he takes care of his dad. But when Roy's gone, RJ won't have an anchor anymore and he's not the kind of person who does well without an anchor."

"What do you mean? You mean—you think he'll kill himself when his dad dies?"

"No, no," said my mother, sounding as though the thought had never occurred to her. "What I mean is he's just like Roy, and your father. No one in that family knows how to take care of themselves. Look how sick they all are—your Gramma, your aunt Katie, Lucy—all of them. But they do know how to get other people to take care of them and they can be very sweet about it, but sometimes...." She let out another sigh. "You're a generous person, Ellie. That's a good thing. Just be careful. You have your own life. Don't forget that."

I couldn't think of what I could say and my mother was quiet, probably waiting to see if I was just going to slam the phone down, emotionally, like my father.

"So," she said finally. "What about you? Can I ask how things are going?"

"I found a place to work."

"That's very good, Ellie. Where?"

"RJ's friends are letting me use their space."

"Is that good? Do you have to share your materials? You never had to do that here."

"They don't do clay. They just have all this stuff."

"Why do they have the stuff if they don't do clay?"

"There was a potter there. He left everything and went to Mexico."

"Why did he do that? Is he coming back?"

"No one seems to think so."

I could tell that she could tell there was a lot more to this, but she wasn't going to push it. At least not that part of it.

"Oh," she said, "that reminds me. One of my patients. I was talking with his mother about you. She's an art agent. Have I told you about her?"

"Once or twice." I knew exactly who she was talking about. This was the anxious anorexic whose son had allergies to his allergy medications. An appointment with them was more like a psychotherapy session, my mother always said, and she finally told the scheduling nurse to give them a double block of time.

"I told her where you were and she said if you're working at a high enough level, you can get into a Santa Fe gallery, but she says you need an agent, even for that."

"Did you show her the pot I made for you?" It was on the windowsill in her office. It was a good little pot, too heartfelt to sell.

"Of course. She said it was lovely."

"Did she offer to represent me?"

"No, sweetheart. Besides, she specializes in paintings. Anyway, her little boy was sick, and obviously we were talking about him."

"Okay."

She was quiet for a while. "Are you getting enough to eat?"

"People feed me all the time. There's no escape. I'll be like a blimp the next time you see me."

"Well," she said, "I guess that's good."

I SPENT the next week tearing apart the old kiln and planning something more efficient. The old kiln was a big catenary arch type, with a chimney that must have been ten feet high before it collapsed. There was a lot of wood ash around the foundation, and I found a pile of disintegrating logs behind the trailer. The mean son-of-a-bitch drunk potter must have been a wood-fire pro, but there was no way I would be able to afford the cords of oak and maple it would take to do long fancy firings. One of my professors in art school had specialized in making kilns out of everyday objects, like barbeque grills, and had even fired pots in a metal shopping cart. I personally had fired pots in ditches filled with scrap lumber and sawdust, but here I was lucky enough to have bricks. All I needed was an efficient design and flammable materials. I could use diesel oil if I had to, propane if I could afford it, and if not, there was always cow shit, goat shit, even coyote shit.

Before I tackled the kiln, I decided it would be prudent to make a few things to test in it. I found a shovel in the shed, went down to the creek and poked around until I found a streak of the same black muck that surrounded the Elephant Butte. I dug up a bucket's worth and chopped in dry clay mix from the shed. I scooped out a couple of big handfuls and wedged them together by hand until I had a sweet, elastic mix. I took a smaller hunk of that, centered it on the wheel, leaned into it, opened it, pulled it into a short, fat cylinder, then a mug-shape, then a tall cup, and finally into a light, graceful form with a neat belly and a graceful neck. I smoothed its lip, stopped the wheel and sat back to look at the pot I had made out of the riverbank. It wasn't what I would have called an "interior statement," but it was a good pot. It wasn't the same as the things I had made before. I might even have called it a correction.

I shaded my eyes at the cottonwoods and the low, cactus-covered hills. The weather was no sunnier, no warmer, no less windy, but I was in a different place now, where everything was calm, focused, and clear.

I MADE a bunch of pots between kiln-building sessions over the next two weeks. Big ones, little ones, tall ones, short ones, fat ones with lids, elegant ones with handles. The clay was slick and plastic, and dried to a kind of charcoal color that I knew would fire to black.

RJ came out early one afternoon to see how I was doing and admired my stacks of productivity. Pots covered the ground in little groups—round over here, tall over there, short with handles, tall with lids and so on.

He walked around the kiln I'd built. It was simple, barrel-shaped, with a six-foot chimney. The kiln walls were as high as my shoulders and mortared with mud. I'd left a section of the wall open so I could walk in to load it, but other than that it was tight, sturdy, facing into the prevailing wind for a good draft. I was proud of it, and if it worked as well as I thought it would, I might make another one just like it.

"I'm firing the kiln tonight," I said. "I have to stay with it, so I won't be home until tomorrow sometime."

"Do you need help?"

"It's more fun with help."

"I'll see if Dad can stand to be without me."

RJ CAME BACK late in the afternoon with Harley, hot dogs and the kids in tow.

"Thought we'd have a cookout," said Harley. "RJ says that's all you did in school. Fire clay and roast wieners."

The kids giggled when he said "wieners." Sunny, who was a girl, held up two huge bags of brand-x marshmallows while the dogs jumped around her.

"I brought dessert!" she said.

I'd met Harley for the first time last week when he came down to see if my fires were going to burn down his farm. Harley wore a battered black leather jacket and had an iron-gray braid down to his waist. From the back he was short and tough-looking, but from the front, except for the jacket, he looked like granddad out of a Norman Rockwell painting. He worked as a car mechanic in T or C, and did handyman work when business was slow. He'd brought a cord and a half of wood up from the barn for me and spent yesterday splitting it. He'd brought a couple of lawn chairs too, because he said he didn't like to see me sitting on the ground.

Hazel came down with ketchup and mustard and paper plates and sent Harley back for beer and fruit juice. RJ got a campfire going and by dusk, the kids were torching marshmallows and feeding their burned, sugary remains to the dogs.

I WASN'T SURE if I wanted to start the kiln with so much craziness, particularly with the dogs chasing each other all over the place, but RJ said I should, that it would be good luck. Everyone waved their juice or beer in the gathering dark, toasting my mud-plastered kiln. I took a flaming branch out of the campfire and squatted by the firebox where kindling and newspaper stuck out. I held the flaming branch up like an Olympic torch and touched the fire to the newspaper. There was a hesitation in the flame, then a suck of air as though the kiln itself was taking a breath. Then a roar, which was the sound of heat rushing up between the pots inside. Smoke puffed up from the chimney, then poured out. Everyone applauded. The dogs ran around and barked. Then the kids turned their attention to flaming their marshmallows and I turned mine to making sure the kiln stayed lit.

HAZEL AND HARLEY took the kids back to the house around ten. They were so full of sugar, I couldn't imagine how they were going to get them into bed. RJ leaned back in his lawn chair with a satisfied sigh. I checked the kiln again. Inside, it glowed cherry red, so hot that I could feel my eyebrows singe when I looked through the peephole.

RJ finished his beer and crumpled the can. "Art school must be a blast. I was wasting my life fighting towel-heads in the Gulf. Who knew?"

I shut the peephole and blundered over to my chair, orange spots floating in front of my eyes. "Did you hate it?" I said.

"Did I hate what?"

"The Marines. The fighting."

He let his head roll back so he was looking up at the sky. "Now why the hell do you want to go and ruin everything by asking me about that?"

"You brought it up."

"I swear, Ellie, you're the cheapest drunk. We talk about this shit every time you've had a couple. Oh, Ellie wants to talk about the Marines. She must have had three or four beers."

"Oh, that's bullshit," I said. "I've been stoned with you and drunk with you and stoned *and* drunk with you and we've never talked about it."

"Yes, we have."

"Yeah?" I said. "When?"

"Remember your dad's funeral?" He waited for me to say something. "Do you?"

I went over to the kiln again, checked the fire, the peep-hole and the draft. I looked out at the cottonwoods. The moon was coming up. I came back to the fire and sat down. "I remember when he died."

"That's important," said RJ. "But what about the funeral?"

"I don't remember the funeral."

He waited a while. "You know why?"

"You got me stoned."

"What do you remember?"

I rubbed my knees, my shins, my ankles under the cuffs of my dirty, smoky jeans. "I remember you and Roy showing up. And Gramma. She yelled at my mom."

"Gramma yelled at everybody," said RJ. "It was her way of showing her love."

"That wasn't love," I said, "I hated her after that."

"That's why you and your mom didn't come to her funeral?"

I shrugged. After my dad was gone my mother told me frankly that she didn't see the point. I hadn't argued.

"Do you remember Granddad's funeral?"

"I was four."

"He drove his rig off a bridge in Arkansas," said RJ. "He caught a whole forest on fire. It burned for days. He made the national news."

"I've heard that."

"He had emphysema and heart disease, just like my dad. He knew he could keel over any time. So he paid a bunch into his life insurance and then took himself out."

"How do you know that?"

"Gramma told me before I went into the Marines. We were both a little toasted. She told me about Granddad and she told me how much she hated the Marines. She told me not to get my ass shot off because I was the sole male heir to the name of Wage."

"Now you're just lying."

"No, she actually said that." RJ cracked another beer, started to offer me one, then changed his mind and put it back in the cooler.

"Don't you worry about your health?" I said. "This stuff obviously runs in the family."

"I worry as much as you do."

"Seriously," I said. "You could do something about it. You know, stop smoking, eat right and exercise and all that."

He sipped contemplatively. "Did it help your dad?"

I was too buzzed to tell if he was joking or being unbelievably mean. "Well," I said, "obviously. He died of something else." RJ didn't say anything, so I said, "What are you going to do when he dies?"

"My dad?" RJ shrugged. "I probably won't be there when it happens."

"What?"

"I mean, it'll probably happen when I'm out. Getting groceries. Or something stupid like that. I'll come home and he'll be stone dead." He took another swig. "It could be happening right now."

"Do you want to call him? Or go home and check on him?"

"That would just be paranoid, Ellie."

"Or sensible?"

"Or obsessing," he said, "over something I can't do anything about. I mean I could hover. I do hover. And then we yell at each other because it makes him feel like a crippled old man."

"He *is* a crippled old man."

RJ sipped his beer. "What does your mom say about him?"

"She says he could last for years." I felt my mother's words pushing their way out of my mouth. "But what're you going to do without an anchor?"

He looked at me and giggled. "An anchor? What am I, a boat? Does your mom think I should get a job with health insurance, and maybe a wife?"

"What's so bad about that?"

"Is that what you think I should do, Cousin Ellie? Do you think I'm a stoner? A loser?"

"RJ…"

"Because everyone else in the family thinks so. And that thing about the wife and the job, that's exactly what my dad says to me, and I'd bet money it's what your mom says to you." He made his voice squeaky and falsely feminine. "'Oh Ellie, those pots are just a waste of time. Why don't you get a *real* job? Why don't you find a *hus*band? You can always make pretty things as a *hob*by.'"

"Oh shut *up*," I said.

"Am I right?"

"Drinking and smoking and making pots aren't the same thing."

"Please," he said, "what're we doing right here, right now?"

"*I'm* firing a kiln."

"And *I'm* taking care of my father." RJ took a long swallow of beer. Neither of us said anything until RJ cleared his throat and got up. "Well," he said, "I gotta take a whiz."

He wandered off and I stayed where I was, listening to the fire roar in the bowels of the kiln. After a while he yelled out of the darkness that he was going home.

MY DAD, who'd been sick for fifteen months when he died, had shrunk from his mighty-bigness until he almost vanished under the blankets. Watching him fade away terrified me, but I didn't want my mother to see it because she was panicking, silently, almost imperceptibly. Every time I looked at her, I could see her mind chasing itself between the things she thought she should have done, to the things she'd promised dad she wouldn't do. I knew he'd made her agree to let him die at home, not in the hospital, to let him go without 'extraordinary measures.' There was nothing foreign in the bedroom—no IVs, not even a heart-rate monitor—just my mother's fingers on the inside of his wrist.

When he went, I remember his exhaustion rising like a vapor from his body. I was so tired and numb I could have slid onto the floor and just lain there. I looked at my mom to see if she was the same but she seemed frozen in place, not even breathing. After a long time one of us said, "I think it's over." I have no idea if it was me or her.

My dad wasn't a metaphorical kind of guy, so we never talked about him "passing on," or "going to his rest," or "being called home," any of the other standard obituary phrases. We called Roy and told him that his brother was dead. Roy called Gramma and over the next two days, the family descended on our house. Gramma was a big, broad-shouldered, white-haired Scots-Irish woman who'd raised four boys and two girls single-handed after her husband died. She'd sent three of her boys to Vietnam, and when two of them were killed within days of each other, she went into the hospital with chest pains. She came out with a quadruple bypass. Gramma had always been a yeller. When things weren't going her way, Gramma yelled. After the bypass, if the yelling wasn't enough she would gasp and grab her chest and everyone in sight would fall into line.

When my father died, Gramma yelled. Roy and RJ showed up and Gramma yelled at them. My aunts and their daughters arrived. More yelling. My dad, dead and unable to see his mother, red in the face with her hands clutching the front of her maroon-colored blouse, refused to come back to life.

And then Gramma turned to my mother and shouted, "You call yourself a *doctor?*"

My mother locked herself in my room until the hour of the funeral. I brought her a bottle of scotch and went off with RJ to find a patch of woods where we could get high. I was stoned out of my mind for my father's funeral. I don't remember any of it. I would feel worse except my mother was pretty tanked herself. After the relatives left, the two of us were standing in the kitchen in the late afternoon. My mother was loading the dishwasher and the house was empty. I remember she had her hair pulled back in a perfect French braid. She was wearing makeup, but it was smudgy on one side, like she'd slept in it. She was in her pajamas with her housecoat on inside out.

EARLY THE NEXT MORNING I put on heavy gloves and pulled a half-dozen bricks out of the kiln wall. A firing in an unproven kiln was often all or nothing. Sometimes the whole load would break because of uneven heating. Other times everything would survive, and the kiln itself was like a gift waiting to be unwrapped. I had time, I told myself. If this didn't work, I could do it again, a different way.

I pulled out enough bricks to make a small window. The pots inside were covered in ash, still smoking. I pulled out a few more bricks and brushed away the ash with my glove. The pots I could see were fine. I reached in with both hands and pulled out the closest one, a small vase, oval-shaped with a small opening in the top, still so hot I could feel it through the gloves. It was black, like a black egg, familiar because I'd made it, but different because the fire changes things. I took out another vase, dusted it off and wiped its surface with spit. The black body had a velvet cast to it, smooth, warm in a way that had nothing to do with the fire. It was good. The firing was good. I didn't have to see anything more to know the whole load was fine. I'd seen some emotional unloadings, with tears or happy screaming, but they were nothing compared to mine, as I danced around the big, blocky kiln with the vases, shrieking to the sky, the mountains, to every art prof who'd ever talked down to me about my interior fucking statements.

HAZEL AND HARLEY admired the pots and seemed to have an appreciation for how well they'd turned out. I took a bowl home to show Roy, knowing I wouldn't get the same reaction.

Roy was at the kitchen table paying bills in the midst of the breakfast dishes. Roy had disability income, but I didn't think it added up to much. RJ was nowhere in sight, and his car wasn't in the driveway.

"Where's RJ?"

"He's getting groceries. You kept him out late."

"Getting groceries," I was starting to understand, was the Roys' euphemism for RJ going out and getting high. I handed my uncle the bowl I'd brought home. It was delicate, thin-rimmed, with spiral throwing marks at the bottom. Its blacks were subtle and thrillingly varied, particularly in sunlight.

"We were having a big old party," I said. "You should have been there."

I gathered up the breakfast dishes. Roy took off his bifocals and held my pot gingerly.

"Looks burnt," he said. "Why didn't you give it some color?"

"I thought it was a pretty black."

"Ain't no one gonna eat their cereal out of a black bowl."

"It's for flowers."

"Ain't no one gonna put their goddamn flowers in a cereal bowl." He put it on the table next to his Corelle coffee cup and saucer. "I guess it's nice," he said finally. "I ain't no judge. You gonna try and sell it up in Santa Fe?"

"I don't know. Not yet."

"Can't think of another place they'd eat their cereal outta black flowerpots." He studied the bowl. "How much you get for a cereal bowl like that?"

"Maybe thirty or forty dollars."

"No shit?"

"No shit."

He shook his head. "Maybe you better show RJ how to do that. He could use a goddamn job."

I poured some more decaf into his cup. "RJ says you yell at him about getting a job."

"Shit yeah, I yell at him. 'Bout lots of things."

"What did RJ do after he got out of the Marines?"

"What do you mean, 'do'?"

"I mean, did he have a job?"

Roy leaned over the bills. "He worked at an auto parts store for a while, and he worked at the marina at the Lake. He tried selling shoes, but that sure as hell didn't work out."

"Why?"

"Well, he nearly punched a guy."

"Why?"

"Oh," he said. "Some people are funny about their feet. You know. Just funny. This guy said the shoes didn't fit, kept being a pain in the ass about it. He drove RJ crazy for an hour or so, and then tried to leave without buying anything. RJ started yellin' and they fired him." He frowned at the checkbook. "It didn't pay anyway. Not like auto parts."

"Why didn't he stay with auto parts?"

"Boring," said Roy. "They wouldn't give him enough hours. He didn't get along with them. I told him it was a good job and he oughta try to stick with it if he could." He shrugged.

"What about at the marina?"

"That was just summer work. I suppose he could've gone

back, but they never called." He eyed me. "Why don't you ask him?"

"He never tells me anything."

"That's because you don't ask him the right way. You can't just hope he'll figure out what you probably might want to ask." Roy snorted. "That's why me and Trisha split up. She thought I should be able to read her mind. And when it became clear to her that I really had no idea what she kinda sorta woulda shoulda wanted from me, she told me to get the hell out."

"Is that why RJ doesn't have a girlfriend? Because he's not telepathic?"

"Shit," said Roy, "he don't have a girlfriend for the same reason he don't have a job. He finds something he doesn't like about it and lets it get out of control in his mind and then he quits."

"But how did he manage in the army?"

"Marines!"

"Sorry, Marines."

"He had to follow orders. If you don't follow orders, you get thrown in the brig." He looked up over his glasses. "And it don't matter how out of control your mind is if you're out in the middle of the desert and assholes are shootin' at you. You just do what you're supposed to fuckin' do."

"He doesn't talk about it."

"He don't talk about much of anything." Roy wrote out a check and stuck it in an envelope with the water and sewage bill. He licked the envelope and put it aside. "Do me a favor," he said, not looking at me. "Don't ever tell him we had this conversation."

RJ CAME HOME in the middle of the afternoon with bloodshot eyes and a couple of bags of groceries. Most of the groceries looked like munchie food. Doritos, popcorn, more cornflakes, and store-bought cookies that couldn't hold a candle to Sherry's. I helped him put the food away. There wasn't a vegetable in sight. The healthiest things were some cans of chicken noodle soup.

"Hey," I said, as RJ and Roy tore open the bag of Doritos. "Want to go to T or C for dinner? I'm buying."

I really wanted to see Larry the potter's work, and his studio was right across the street from Maria's Tortillas, a T or C institution. Maybe I'd run into him and we could talk about the Santa Fe clay scene.

RJ looked up from the chips, fingers and lips coated with orange dust. "Sure!" he said. "We could have burgers at the bar."

The bar was Dan's, a sort of fake western dive with décor appropriate for tourists. I'd never liked their food.

"Let's go for Mexican," I said. "How about Maria's?"

"Can't eat that Mexican food no more," said Roy, and rubbed his chest as though he had heartburn just thinking about it. "Don't know how anyone can."

"You could get a steak," said RJ. "I know they have steak. Steak and eggs."

Roy looked like he really wanted to. "I'd have to lug around the goddamn oxygen tank."

"Steak and eggs," said RJ, like he was offering something tasty to a pet.

Roy gave an unhappy shrug. "Just bring me something. You kids have fun," he said, without conviction.

RJ AND I got to Maria's around six that evening, during the dinner rush. In the cool of the evening, the locals sat at tables on the sidewalk, mingling with college students with school sweatshirts from California and back east. The roasted-corn smell of hot tortillas filled the street. Maria's Tortillas sat across the street from Larry's studio, in a row of storefronts that included a Yoga Center, a Marxist bookstore, and a tie-dye boutique.

A small crowd was gathered in front of Larry's. RJ and I had to squeeze in to see the display, which was divided in to two parts: functional dinnerware on one side—a ten-piece place setting, beautifully thrown, laid out on a white linen tablecloth. On the other side of the display window was stuff like what'd made it to the gallery up north. It was dinnerware, too—I could tell by the way it was arranged. The forms were tinted in turquoise, lusciously abstract. They were fragile and luminous, and though one might have been a soup tureen and one might have been a teapot, they were useless for anything but display. If I'd ever seen an "interior statement," these were definitely that.

"Wow," I said. "Wow, those are beautiful."

"Wow," said RJ. "I'm starving. Let's eat."

SEEING LARRY'S STUFF inspired me. It was February now, and truly winter, which came to the desert in the form of rain. I invested in blue plastic tarps and Harley built me a shelter out of two by fours with a corrugated metal roof. We dragged the potter's wheel under it just as huge black clouds rolled in from the west, but I'd already decided I wasn't going to make any more pots. I wasn't sure what I was going to do, but it wasn't going to be the same old containers. Harley had left me a nice-sized blunt, "on the house," and even though it was still morning, I smoked a little, just to lubricate my mind.

The weed was excellent and smooth. As the golden buzz enveloped me, I pushed away the urge to do nothing. I had plenty of clay in my little shelter and I'd never made anything out of clay while I was stoned. As high as I was, there was no anxiety about "interior statements." I just started making stuff. The kind of stuff that no one was ever going to see.

I crimped the clay and flattened it and made it into things that weren't containers. One squashed-together form made me think of Roy. Another one, misshapen and non-functional, was RJ. A thing like a pancake ended up squared at the edges like a box, and seemed to be Sherry. The golden buzz projected me into an afternoon of creating emotional objects that embodied my grad school rejections. Useless classes with clueless profs who handed out stupid, purely subjective grades. *Be original,* they'd said to me one-on-one, during my after-class critiques. *Find what means something to you and translate that into your own, personal statement.* One of them actually said to me, *maybe you're just too young to know what's inside you.* I'd said, full of hostility and a horrible sense that I'd wasted a ton of tuition money, *Maybe you're being too subjective.* This prof, a woman with work in galleries all over the world, replied coolly, *Maybe you should take a break and come back to school in a couple of years.*

I made a thing called *Subjectivity* and hurled it into the cottonwoods.

It started to rain but I didn't care. I made things about winters in Baltimore. It rained harder and lightning flashed around me. I took a few more tokes off Harley's weed and got on the wheel. I made a whole bunch of pots, all hideous, and nothing at all like Larry's transcendental work in Truth or Consequences. I inflicted wounds on them with wet metal potters' tools and threw them out into the rain to punish them for their ugliness.

I made a pot about my mother, and how she had failed to save my father. It sagged on the wheel, too wet to hold its own weight, and collapsed, through no fault of its own. From that soggy heap I made a pot about my dad, rising from a mighty-bigness in the body, to the thinnest neck I had ever thrown. I sat back to look at it and discovered I was crying. I put my clay-covered hands over my face and let myself sob, wiping my cheeks until I was covered in black grit.

HOURS LATER, the buzz had thinned and it was getting dark. Wind shoved rain under my little shelter and I realized I had no way to get back to the Roys without getting drenched. I was hungry. I was out of clay. I was soaked. The blunt was wet and so were the matches. I spread a blue tarp over everything I hadn't destroyed—black clay bodies and emotional wreckage. Punctuated by lightning, the tarp looked like the surface of a strange plastic sea. I left everything behind and walked the soaking quarter-mile to Hazel and Harley's and found RJ there, looking surprised to see me.

THE NEXT DAY it only drizzled and I made RJ drop me off at the end of Harley's driveway. No one was home. I walked out to the back forty, greeted by saturated cacti, flowering as fast as they could, swarms of insects and hysterically happy birds.

I trudged around the edge of the hollow, past the bowed branches of the cottonwoods. I really couldn't remember what I'd made. All the emotion I'd poured into my work yesterday had become a swollen feeling under my eyes. When I pulled the blue tarp back, I wasn't surprised to see that, objectively, I had made lumps. The only thing that was still recognizable was the pot that was my dad, its thin, vanishing neck wavering high above the soft, turdish forms of everything else. I sat down in a damp lawn chair. I'd thrown half my clay into the bushes and it would take all day to make more. I tried to decide if I felt better for this catharsis, but was too hungover to reach a definite conclusion. So I got up, got the shovel, and dug, and mixed, and let my mind go blank.

That afternoon and over the next few days, I tried to channel Larry's success into my next batch of pots and came up with some nice variations. I made sure not to copy anything I'd seen of his and nothing I made was especially elegant, but even when I made myself be critical, I could appreciate my own skill and almost—*almost*—see the creative direction I needed to go. They looked good. If they all came out of the fire in one piece, some of them might be good enough get into a local gallery. If not, I could just start over. That kind of thinking would've sent me into a spiral of misery in Baltimore, where anything that didn't feel like progress had to be a failure. Here, the immense, indifferent, vast, eternal, implacable desert didn't give a shit if I spent months—or years—trying to find my artistic direction. Roy and RJ and Hazel and Harley didn't care if I sold anything in Santa Fe, ever. I could relax and let inspiration come in its own time.

I ASKED RJ to help me fire the next load and he agreed when I promised not to make him talk about the Marines. It was a dry day for a change, and I spent it loading the kiln, stacking and angling with obsessive precision. I arranged deadfall and dry cactus in the mouth of the kiln. RJ didn't show up. It got darker and darker. He still didn't show. I decided to hell with him and lit the kiln just as it started to rain again.

Rain or not, fire rushed inside the kiln as soon as I set a match to it. It inhaled the firewood at its mouth. It breathed heat and exhaled a fine white smoke from the chimney. I wrapped myself in a plastic tarp and sat far enough back to not catch fire myself. The wind picked up. The draft increased with the wind and I piled in more wood. By about eleven, the kiln was so hot it practically glowed. Rain hissed when it hit the hot bricks. Did I have a feeling about this firing? I did have a feeling about this firing. It was a good, hot, steady roaring feeling. White smoke rose against the rain, blackness pressed down on the barrel of heat and fire and the mad patterns of light in the firebox. There was a steady inward suck of air. The kiln was transforming everything inside from common earth to something immortal and pure.

AROUND MIDNIGHT, I heard an engine in the near distance and the squeak of old suspension as someone drove through the mud and scrub. I saw headlights and assumed it was RJ, but when I got up to shout *hey asshole!* in the friendliest possible way, the car turned into Hazel's truck, with Hazel rolling down the window, squinting into the rain.

"Where's RJ?" she hollered.

"No idea!" I ran over to the truck, still draped in blue plastic. "What's wrong?"

"Sherry called. She says Roy's had a heart attack." She leaned over to shove the passenger door open. "Get in!"

Stupidly, I looked back at the fire in the kiln, which would die without me.

"Get *in*!" said Hazel. I shed my tarp and got in.

SHE LENT ME her truck and I drove to the Roys as fast as I could. The rain had stopped for the moment and I saw the ambulance in the front yard as I pulled in. There was no sign of RJ or his car. I ran into the house expecting the very worst, but instead, the ambulance guys were standing around. Roy was still in his recliner. Sherry was on the phone. The TV was on. Everything seemed just this side of normal except that Roy was panting into an oxygen mask.

"What's happening?" I said.

"Ain't nothin happening," said Roy, and coughed, hard and painfully.

"Hazel said you had a heart attack!"

Sherry looked up from the phone. "I told her I thought it *might* be a heart attack. Where's RJ?"

"I don't know." I turned to the ambulance guys. Both smelled of cigarettes. Both were Indians. Neither of them looked worried. "Why aren't you taking him to the hospital?" I demanded.

"He doesn't want to go," said one.

"Can't you *make* him go?"

"Sir," the other one said to Roy, "you sure you don't want to come with us?"

Roy shoved himself upright in the chair and heaved himself to his feet, red in the face, breathless. He yanked off the oxygen mask. *"I ain't goin' to the goddamn hospital!"*

Sherry tightened her mouth and frowned at the telephone.

Roy sank into the chair again and pressed the mask over his nose and mouth. In that moment, I could almost see how much time he had left. All I could think of was my dad.

The ambulance guys looked at me. "Guess he doesn't want to go."

I could understand that, but only objectively. Subjectively I needed to sit down and wipe my eyes.

Sherry, turned back to the phone, nodded and scribbled. "Thank you, doctor. We'll be there first thing in the morning." She hung up. "You're supposed to keep the oxygen turned up."

Roy glanced at the tank as though it could never be turned up far enough.

Sherry came over to me and the ambulance guys. "Sorry to drag you boys out here. You want some coffee before you go? Some cookies?"

They declined and left. For a minute, there was no sound but the hiss of Roy's oxygen and rain against the windows.

"You should go home," I said to Sherry, blocking out all thoughts of my kiln. "I'll make sure he's okay."

She looked reluctant, but left.

Roy looked at me helplessly, and at that moment, I felt like I'd lived there forever—or maybe I *would* live here forever—and my mother had the social protocols all wrong.

"Where were you?" he gasped accusingly.

I was smoky and filthy. I thought it was obvious where I'd been. "Firing," I said.

He blinked in resignation. "You're out gettin' high, just like him."

A car pulled into the gravel driveway, and in a minute, RJ strolled in.

"What's everybody doing up?" He gave me a loopy grin. "Isn't it, like, one in the morning? Hey, how'd your firing go?"

"Jesus Christ," I said, "where the fuck have you been?"

RJ angled a thumb over his shoulder, eyes wide, blood-shot. "Just...out."

"Your dad almost had a heart attack," I shouted. "The ambulance was here! Hazel had to come and get me because no one could find *you!*"

"But I was just..." RJ took a step back toward the door. "I was out by the lake. Hell, I haven't been gone for more than an hour."

I felt my father's face-punching rage fill me up and my mother's quiet stability vanish, like mud in the rain. "You're so full of *shit!*" I yelled, just like a true-born Wage, just like Gramma. "You don't care about anything, or anyone. You're just high all the time! You're *so* full of shit, you don't even care if he *dies!*" I waved an arm at Roy, who had sunk deeper into the recliner. "You're supposed to be taking *care* of him. What the hell is *wrong* with you?"

RJ stared at me like he'd never seen me before. I could tell his buzz had been blasted away. He glanced at his father and back at me. He went to sit on the sofa, next to the recliner.

"You okay, Dad?" he said.

"Fuck you," whispered Roy. "I'm fine."

RJ put his fists between his knees and looked at me, like he would sit right there until hell froze over.

I went into Roy's bedroom but left the door open. I was filthy and smoky and I sat on the floor. Before long snoring filled the house.

I thought about my kiln. It hadn't been hot enough for long enough. As it cooled, my pots would be stranded between being earth and immortal. Some would crumble back into dirt. Some might be able to take a second round of blazing heat. Mostly I would have to start again. I had time, I told myself and lay on the floor. It was past two in the morning. Snoring made the floor vibrate. The vibration made me want to cry. I waited a long and awful hour and finally got up to check on Roy.

RJ was lying on the sofa now, sound asleep.

I leaned over Roy. His throat shuddered with the effort of inhaling. His face was sunken around his eyes and cheekbones. He looked worn out, almost bruised with the effort of staying alive. He looked like my father.

I took a blanket, went out to Hazel's truck and curled up in the truck bed with sacks of animal feed. The silence was a relief. I went to sleep, and woke up almost immediately. The neighborhood dogs were going nuts. I sat up, chilled under a sky full of stars. The moon was almost full, waning over the western mountains and cast hard blue shadows. Coyote voices floated over everything in nuanced canine harmonies.

Ooooooooooooowooooooowooowoo.

The dogs up and down the street barked madly, unmusically.

I heard the front door open. I expected RJ, but it was Roy. He turned toward the truck, and in the moonlight, I saw a gun in his hand.

"Who's out here?" he wheezed.

I waved my arms over my head. "Just me!"

Roy dropped into a lawn chair. I scrambled out of the truck. He wasn't wearing his cannula. He could hardly breathe. He was holding the gun in his lap. Where did he keep it that he could have put his hands on it so fast? In the recesses of his recliner? I started for the door to get RJ, but Roy waved me back.

"Wait," he panted. "Wait a goddamned minute."

The coyotes wailed again. The dogs let loose a barrage of pointless racket.

"They're coming down," said Roy. "Can you hear?"

Lights went on down the street. Someone yelled at their dog to shut the hell up. I looked toward the gate expecting to see coyotes any minute. All I could see was my own breath.

"You should get inside," I said.

"What're you doing out here?" Roy demanded.

"The snoring," I said. "I couldn't sleep."

"Thought you were down with RJ's hippie friends." He was winded and hoarse. "You're spendin' a lot of time there."

"I'm working out there. It takes a lot of time."

"You're spendin' nights."

"Just once in a while."

"Look," said Roy, and now he sounded angry. It was the

kind of gasping anger I'd almost been able to hear when he and RJ fought. "You want to move out, you go ahead and move out. But I ain't gonna tell your ma you moved into some goddamn dump because you couldn't get any sleep around here."

"I won't move into a dump."

"And I don't want you livin' by yourself."

"RJ told me to get a dog."

"I mean another person, girl."

"Like who?"

"Like a boyfriend. You should find one." He was gasping. "Just stay away from them Mexican fellas. And the Indians. None of 'em ever worked a lick in their lives. You'll just end up supporting 'em and having babies."

I took a step toward the door but he grabbed my wrist.

"You've never had any trouble," said Roy. "You don't know what trouble is. A young girl alone. Old folks. Sick folks. There's predators out there." He gripped the gun. He was shivering. "You got to watch out for yourself. No one's going to do it for you. Didn't your dad teach you anything?"

I didn't know what to say. "I'll get RJ."

"You ain't sleeping in the back of a goddamn truck," he said, and I thought he might burst into tears.

The front door opened and RJ came out. "Dad? What're the hell're you doing?"

Roy toughened his voice. "We're waiting for the goddamn coyotes."

"The hell you are." RJ pulled him out of the lawn chair and eyed me. "They're not coming. They hear voices and they're gone."

He took his father inside. The dogs had stopped barking but I shuffled down to the gate and looked anyway. First I thought RJ was right, and then I saw them. Three coyotes sat on the other side of the dirt road, tongues lolling, breath coming out in hot puffs. They looked at me. I stared back through the chain-link, waiting for the hairs to raise on the back of my neck, waiting for the thrill of looking into the wild eyes. What I saw instead was an animal expectation, like they thought I would open the gate and let them in. They sat and stared at me, freezing in my socks as though I was a goat on a ledge, on the verge of leaving the safety of my shrinking island.

The door opened behind me. RJ came out. "What's going on?"

The coyotes peed on the sagebrush and trotted off into the dark. The moonlight didn't even show paw prints where they'd been.

"I saw them," I shouted back, and walked up to the house over the sharp gravel. I didn't say, *They're stalking the weak and sick.*

He had his bottle of Jack Daniels and took a long swallow. He offered me the bottle but I shook my head. I started to go inside, out of the cold, but RJ caught my shoulder.

"Look," he said. "We need to talk."

"About what?" I said coldly. "I think I said everything I needed to say."

"But I didn't," said RJ. He turned me, by the shoulder, to face him. "You know how my dad is. Even if I'd been here—even if it'd been worse—he doesn't want me to call an ambulance. Okay? He just wants to be left alone. So even if

I'd been right next to him, nothing would be any different right now." He tilted his head in an unsure angle. "We've talked about it. You know. No extraordinary measures. You know. Like your dad. And your mom."

"Being home with a sick person isn't an extraordinary measure," I said, angry again.

"Just listen," he said. "When your dad got sick, we all said to each other, 'Well, Deborah's a doctor. Isn't that great? He'll be fine.'" He put down the Jack Daniels and took out a pack of cigarettes. "He died. She was right next to him."

"She's a pediatrician," I said, my voice shaking. "That means *little kids*."

He lit the cigarette with unsteady hands. "Did you ever ask her if there was something more she could have done?"

I could feel Gramma's vehemence filling my throat again. "What was I supposed to say?"

"How about, 'Mom, maybe you're not doing enough because your husband's about to croak.' I mean did you ever say anything like that?"

I felt my mouth hang open. "You're exactly what everyone says you are."

"What's that?" He took a deep drag. "A failure? You should know."

I turned and walked away. I went in and got my shoes, came back out, shoved past him and got into Hazel's pickup. I slammed the door as hard as I could.

"I'm not going anywhere, Ellie," RJ shouted after me as I pulled out. "What about *you?*"

I managed to get out of the driveway without hitting anything before I realized I hadn't turned on the headlights. I wiped the tears out of my eyes and headed for the lake, then changed my mind and wove down the highway, heading for my kiln.

I PARKED the truck at Harley and Hazel's, left the keys in the ignition and made my way down the quarter mile of damp, dark isolation. As I walked, I tried to make some resolutions for myself. I couldn't stay with the Roys and I couldn't afford to move out. I didn't have enough money to establish myself here. If I went back to Baltimore, I might have enough money left to pick up where I'd left off. The look I would see on my mother's face when I dragged myself home in defeat made me cry like a grad school reject.

The kiln was still smoking. I could smell it and feel the heat left in it, but the fire in its mouth was out. I used half a box of matches to get it lit and huddled beside its brick body. The dampness in the wind made the weather frigid. I wrapped myself in plastic but it was anything but comforting. The fire finally caught. The kiln groaned and smoked. I fed it more wood, crouched at its mouth, veiled in blue plastic as I waited for the *pop-pop-pop* of ceramic self-destruction.

By noon I was out of firewood. I went back to Hazel's for a shower and a bowl of cereal. No one was home. I curled up in Sunny's bed and slept until Hazel came home around five and asked what was going on. I told her my day-old news while she warmed dinner for me. I told her I'd fired the kiln but couldn't open it until morning.

She sat down across from me with a cup of chamomile and began talking about her daughter's troubles with drugs and the law. I knew there was some metaphorical message in whatever she was saying and how it pertained to me, or RJ, or to us both. She dipped the tea bag in and out of the steaming water. I stared at the cup, not really listening. It was a beautiful cup, cobalt-colored with a handle so delicate that the only thing holding it in place was the thumbprint of its absent maker. Whatever Hazel was saying was eclipsed by the cup. Steam rose, clouding its marvelous blues. She took a sip. The cup fit her hands and lips, its body meant only to be held between palms or fingers, its mouth made to fit the drinker's, fulfilling its muddy destiny of being created simply to contain.

I SLEPT on the couch that night, and woke up to an empty house. Outside, the peacocks eyed me with suspicion but the dogs followed happily as I walked out to the back forty, to whatever was waiting for me. It was a cloudy morning with signs and portents going both ways. No visible sun, which was bad, but the weather was warmer, which was good. Hawks rode the rising winds high overhead, which was good, but without the sun behind them, they had none of that golden mythos and might as well have been vultures. Which was bad. By the time I got to the kiln I was ready to throw up.

I pulled away bricks one by one, ready to join the art school weepers I had so disdained. Inside, the first pot was in pieces, but the one next to it, amazingly, had withstood its neighbor's explosion and was fine. I pulled down the rest of the wall. Most of the pots were fine. They glowed with velvety black confidence. Out by myself on a wet afternoon in the desert, I did a crazy-person victory dance, shrieking and flinging broken, blown-up shards as offerings to the gods of failure. I screamed at the goats, too stupid to stay in a safe place, and to RJ too stupid to know who was on his side, and to my mother, my poor mother, who couldn't have done any more than she had done.

I HAD THE KILN unloaded by afternoon and packed the ten best pots in a box. I took them down to the house, where I found Harley backing out of the garage. Hazel's truck was gone, and he said she'd taken the kids to the dollar store in Elephant Butte. He was on his way to T or C.

"Can I get a ride with you?"

"Where you headed?"

I opened one flap of the box so he could see. "To see that potter guy," I said. "The one who got a show in Santa Fe."

HARLEY DROPPED me off at Larry's storefront studio, across from Maria's Tortillas. The street was empty and Larry's shop was locked up tight. I looked at his sign that listed the days he was open and realized I had no idea what day it was, much less the time. I stared at his work through the big glass window until I noticed my own reflection. Damp hair, sooty face, puffy eyes, big box. I probably smelled like a campfire. Suddenly I felt exhausted and hungry. I had five bucks in my pocket, which was enough for the burrito platter at Maria's. I wasn't sure how I would get back to the Roys, or even if I should. I would eat, then think.

I saw Larry just paying his bill at the counter as I walked in. He looked at me and gave a little nod, like he could see that I recognized him and knew all about his achievements.

"Hey," he said.

"Hey," I said. "Congratulations on, um, everything."

"Thanks." He stuffed his wallet into his pocket. "Have you been over to the shop?"

I nodded. "Your work is amazing."

"Thanks." He gave me a sort of searching look. "You know," he said, "either you've just run out of a burning house or you've been firing."

"Oh," I said. "Oh, firing. I've been making pots up there on the east side of the dam. I built a kiln." I was holding the box of pots so tightly that the cardboard was beginning to crumple. I felt like I'd been living in a foreign country for months, and here I was, babbling to the first person who spoke my language. "I brought some of them with me. I wanted to show you."

"A lot of people've been bringing me things they think would sell in Santa Fe."

"I'll bet."

"They're in that box?"

He guided me to a table and I pulled the pots out of the box, one by one. He spent a lot of time handling them. I could tell he liked them by the way he cradled them.

"You made the clay yourself," he said.

"I mixed it with some other stuff, but yeah, it's ninety percent riverbank."

Larry turned the vase that was my father around in his hands. "Not everything that goes to Santa Fe does well in Santa Fe. Take it from me."

"What do you think about these?"

He raised an eyebrow and gave me back the vase. "I'm

going up tomorrow. Want to come along? I can introduce you to some people."

I swallowed. "Okay," I said. "Okay."

"You'll have to clean yourself up a little," he said.

I let out a laugh. "Sure," I said. "Sure."

WE EXCHANGED phone numbers, and when he was gone I went outside again and stood on the sidewalk in the cool brightness of the desert afternoon. I had no clear plan on how to get back to the Roys. It was five miles, more or less, to their house. I could walk it and get there before dark, but not with a box of pots.

I started down the street, past the Yoga Center and the Marxist Bookstore and the tie-dye emporium. The student tourists were gone and the snowbirds, in their sunglasses and floral shirts had returned, sparsely now, but soon in droves. I passed an elderly couple scrutinizing the "Indian Crafts" through a shop window, a half dozen ladies drinking cocktails at a sidewalk café table. Further on, two women wearing turquoise necklaces and cowboy hats stood outside a real estate office making notes of the listings in the window. I stopped, just to have a look. A lot of the fliers were for acreage, a few for new houses at astronomical prices. Then down at the bottom of the window I saw the turquoise trailer around the corner from the Roys.

8 x 45, 1958 American Mobile Home on quarter acre lot. Rustic cabin style. Much of the interior is unfinished. $1,000 Or Best Offer

IT WAS a piece of crap, just like Roy had said, but it really didn't matter. It was a piece of crap I could put a down payment on, in the right place, at the right time. I couldn't spend my days out at Hazel and Harley's anymore. It was too hard to get home if something went wrong. RJ wasn't dependable, and RJ knew that better than anyone.

The real estate office was open, and I walked straight in, dirty clothes, smoky hair, wild eyes, box of pots.

The man behind the nearest desk looked at me over his glasses, like he'd seen weirder things. "Can I help you, miss?"

"The trailer," I said. "The one for a thousand bucks. Can you take me out to see it?"

"Sure." He opened a drawer and took out a ring of keys. "You should know, though, the plumbing on that property's going to need a lot of work."

"Does it have running water?" I said. "Electricity?"

"Yes, but the septic system—"

"Doesn't matter," I said. "I'll worry about that later."

We put the pots in the back seat of his silver Camry. He held the door for me, and the two of us drove east, turning onto the state highway that separated T or C from the park.

In the arid distance, the elephant rose from the shrinking lake, its trunk trailing into the sandbar. The water was even lower than when RJ and I had walked down there in January. Not even a puddle showed along the sandbar.

From the highway, the lakeshore gleamed in rusty iron tones. The town of Elephant Butte shimmered in the afternoon. To the west, the mountains seemed flat in the hard sunlight, snowless and gray. Vultures circled on the rising wind and I shaded my eyes at the remains of the lake, which had never belonged here. The cabin cruisers coming down the highway on trailers from Albuquerque hadn't belonged here.

The goats certainly hadn't.

Acknowledgements

THANK YOU, first of all, to the Washington Writers Publishing House, who picked my collection as a winner for their annual competition. Thanks for making this an unforgettable experience. I look forward to working with all of you in the years to come.

Thank you to cover artist, Jodi Hoover, and Designer, Nett Smith for making such a gorgeous book.

Thanks to my amazing writing group, Ellen, Stephanie, and Emily, who read these stories over and over and over, and never complain about my incessant demands on their time.

Of course, no acknowledgement is complete without thanking my wife, Vicki, who has somehow endured me and my writing dreams for forty years. You are my love.

My profound thanks to Olga Zilberbourg, who was responsible for the first publication of three of these stories in Narrative Magazine, and to Richard Peabody, who nominated The Witch Bottle for a Pushcart when he published it in Gargoyle.

About the Author

SUZANNE FELDMAN graduated from the Maryland Institute College of Art in 1981 and received a Masters Degree in Creative Writing from Johns Hopkins University in 2004. She is the author of three science fiction novels under her pen name, Severna Park. She received a Nebula Award in 2001 for her short fiction and the Editors Prize for fiction in 2005 at The Missouri Review. She has had stories published in Narrative Magazine, including *The Lapedo Child* which was selected as one of the year's best (2013). Her short story collection, *The Cure For Everything* was awarded the International Rubery Prize for fiction, 2014. Her novel *Absalom's Daughters* (Holt, 2016) received a starred review in Kirkus. Her short story *The Witch Bottle* (Gargoyle Magazine 2016) was nominated for a Pushcart Prize. She was a Walter Dakin Fellow at the Sewanee Writers Conference in 2019. Her latest novel, *Sisters of the Great War,* (Mira/HarperCollins, 2021) has been nominated for a Lambda Literary Award. In 2022 she was awarded her third grant from the Maryland State Arts Council and won The Washington Writers' Publishing House Fiction Prize for her short story collection, The Witch Bottle.

She can be reached through her website SuzanneFeldman.net

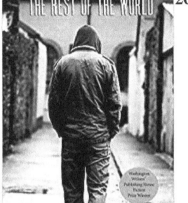
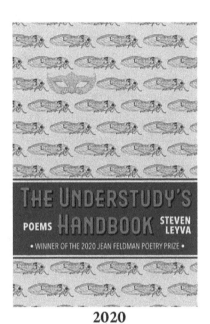

WWPH is an independent, nonprofit, cooperative press founded in 1975. Our mission is to publish and celebrate writers from DC, Maryland, and Virginia. To learn more about our fiction, poetry, and creative nonfiction manuscript contests, our bi-weekly literary journal, and to purchase more WWPH books, please visit:

www.washingtonwriters.org

Follow us on:
Twitter@wwphpress
Facebook@WWPH
Instagram@writingfromWWPH

Contact us at:
wwphpress@gmail.com

PROUD MEMBER

COMMUNITY OF LITERARY MAGAZINES & PRESSES
W W W . C L M P . O R G

WWPH is a proud recipient of a
Creativity Grant from

CPSIA information can be obtained
at www.ICGtesting.com
Printed in the USA
JSHW021319120622
26870JS00001B/3